THE PIKE RIVER PHANTOM

OTHER BOOKS BY BETTY REN WRIGHT

THE PIKE RIVER PHANTOM

Betty Ren Wright

AN
APPLE
PAPERBACK

SCHOLASTIC INC.
New York Toronto London Auckland Sydney

ISBN 0-590-42808-X

12 11 10 9 8 7   5/9

Printed in the U.S.A.   40

First Scholastic printing, June 1990

Dedicated to ANNE POWERS SCHWARTZ
and to ARTHUR R. TOFTE,
friends of my heart

THE PIKE RIVER PHANTOM

CHAPTER 1

Charlie shivered as he started up the porch steps of the house. He could still hear the bees humming cozily in the overgrown garden. He could still taste the raspberries he'd sampled just outside the gate. He could smell the piney woods. But bees and berries, sun and pines, seemed to be tilting away from him, slipping and sliding toward someplace else.

Crazy, he thought. *Who needs this old dump?* But his feet went on climbing the steps, and his hand lifted the rusty bulldog-head knocker. One knock, he promised himself, and then he'd head back to town. He had already started to turn away when the door opened.

"What do you want, boy?"

The woman was tall, at least six feet, and very straight. Her skin was creased and brown, and the black hair hitched behind her ears was heavily streaked with gray. She was old, but it wasn't the round, dimply oldness of Charlie's Grandma Lou. This woman looked as if she'd been dried in the sun for a couple of hundred years.

"Well?" She seemed to scrape up the single word from deep in her chest. Her eyes glittered like wet stones as she stared down at Charlie. No, he thought uneasily, she wasn't staring *at* him exactly. It was as if she were staring *through* him and seeing something stupid or silly he hadn't even known was there.

A drop of sweat rolled between his eyes and down the side of his nose. He struggled to remember the sales pitch he'd been repeating at different doorways all morning. "C-Candy?" he stammered finally, his voice shooting up in the way he hated. "Do you want to buy some candy?"

"Why are you selling candy?" The woman sounded curious. "Are you poor?"

Charlie reached into the canvas sack he carried, glad of an excuse to turn away from those shining eyes. "It's for my cousin Rachel's school," he mumbled, holding up a candy bar. "Pike River Middle School. The Pike River Middle School band, I mean. They get to play at a college football game in Madison next fall if they raise enough money for the bus and the motel and . . . stuff." His explanation faded off. It was clear that the old lady wasn't interested in his answer to her question. She was looking over his head, toward the woods, as if she'd forgotten he was there.

"You come from Pike River," she stated. "What's it like now?"

"It's okay." *What did she expect to hear?* he wondered. She must have lived here a lot longer than he had. "I just moved to Pike River from Milwaukee a couple of weeks ago, so—" He took a deep breath. "About the candy. It's really good. Chocolate with almonds."

She plucked the bar from his fingers. "I used to like chocolate," she said. She dropped the candy into the pocket of her ragged gray sweater and smiled at him meanly.

"That's a dollar," Charlie said, "a dollar a bar."

The woman continued to smile. "But I don't have any dollars," she said. "I don't have any money at all." *And what are you going to do about it?* She didn't say that, but Charlie felt the words hanging in the air.

He remembered the touch of her dry fingers as they'd closed around the candy bar. "I can come back for the money tomorrow," he said. But he knew he wouldn't. It had been a waste of time to come way out here, nearly a mile from the center of town. The mailbox on the highway suggested there might be a customer no one else had thought of, but it had been a mistake to bother.

"I won't have money tomorrow either." The woman

bent suddenly and pushed her face close to Charlie's. She smelled like dead flowers. "Now, who is it you look like?" she asked in a mocking tone. "Big eyes, big mouth, big ears—you take after somebody I know. Saw it as soon as you came out of the woods. What's your name, boy?"

"Charlie. Charles James Hocking." He considered snatching the candy bar from the sagging sweater-pocket. A person had a right to take back what was stolen, didn't he?

"You Will Hocking's little brother?"

"He's my grandpa!"

The woman looked startled, then she sniffed. "Grandpa?" she repeated. "Don't be silly! Will is a nice enough boy—better than most in the town. You tell your brother the *real* Sunbonnet Queen says hello."

Charlie started to ask what she meant, then leaped backward as the door was slammed in his face. She'd almost knocked him off his feet! For a moment he stood there, staring at the bulldog knocker inches from his nose. He could hear the woman laugh on the other side of the door. Then he raced down the steps, across the garden, through the falling-down gate, and into the woods.

When he finally slowed to a walk, he was panting hard. The road through the woods had seemed spookily dark when he'd passed through on his way to the clearing, but now he welcomed the shelter of the trees. They cut off his view of the old house and muted the laughter that followed him.

Laurel Avenue was lined with maples, planted when the street was new thirty years ago. The houses were mostly ranches, some with attached garages and some without. Grandpa Will's had a garage, and the connecting breezeway had been screened in to make a little room. Our summer dining room, Grandma Lou called it. Beyond it were the kitchen, the real dining room, the living room, two bedrooms, and a den. Grandpa and Grandma had the big bedroom, and Rachel had the other one. She was staying in Pike River while her missionary parents were in Africa.

Charlie and his father shared a fold-out bed in the den.

"It's not so convenient, but I suppose it'll do," Grandma Lou had said a little doubtfully, when she'd welcomed them. "We don't have a lot of space here, but we surely do love to have our family with us."

Charlie didn't mind a bedroom that wasn't really a bedroom; he was used to that. Back in Milwaukee, he'd lived with his aunt Laura and had slept on her living-room couch all the years that his father was away. Actually, he'd gone to sleep every night in Aunt Laura's bed, and when she finished watching the ten o'clock news she'd got him up and led him, half awake, out to the couch. Sleeping in his grandparents' den was almost like having a regular bedroom.

The house was quiet when Charlie let himself in. He stopped in the kitchen for a glass of milk, then wandered down the hall to Rachel's room. He had dropped the canvas candy-bag on her desk chair and was just reaching into his pocket for the money he'd collected when the back door slammed and quick steps sounded in the hall. Rachel appeared in the doorway.

"What are you doing in my bedroom, Charlie Hocking? My bedroom is private. I've told you that a million times!" She was slim, with dark brown hair, and snapping brown eyes like Grandma Lou's.

"How could you tell me a million times?" Charlie retorted. "I've only been living here for two weeks. If you told me a million times, that would be one million divided by fourteen days, and that would be—"

"Forget it." Rachel threw herself on the bed and kicked off her shoes. "Just tell me what you want. I don't have time for children today."

"Children!" Charlie wondered if all girls were as annoying as this one. If they were, he'd be a bachelor forever. "You're only thirteen—one lousy year older than I am."

"It hasn't been a lousy year," Rachel said smugly. "It's been the best year of my life. So far. I'm in Middle School. I'm president of my class. I wear a bra." Her glance fell on the canvas bag. "So how many candy bars did you sell?"

"Twelve," Charlie said, relieved at the change of subject. "One lady bought three, and she gave me an extra fifty cents for myself." He pulled a handful of bills from his pocket and dropped them on the bed.

"Well, that's very good." Rachel sounded surprised and pleased. "That's really not bad at all. I told you—a child could do it." She grinned at him, then reached across the bed to snag the canvas bag with a toe. "Hey!" she exclaimed, peering into its depths. "I gave you fifteen bars, and there are two left. You sold twelve—where's the other one?"

Charlie kicked the leg of the desk chair. He wasn't ready to talk about the strange old lady in the house in the woods—certainly not to Rachel. He couldn't tell her that he'd let the woman take a candy bar without paying for it. "What *did* you do?" she'd moan. "What did you say to her? Why didn't you make her give it back, you silly baby?"

He tried an explanation that was at least partly the truth. "There was this old lady," he said. "She didn't have any money, but I think she's going to pay me later. . . ." It sounded weak, even to him.

Rachel sat up and glared. "I'll just bet," she said, her voice heavy with sarcasm. "You ate it, didn't you? That's the same as stealing, Charlie Hocking. You ought to be ashamed."

Charlie clenched his fists. "I didn't steal it!" he yelled. "I'll pay for it myself, if you're going to make a big deal out of it—but I didn't steal it!" He reached into his shirt pocket and pulled out two dimes and the fifty-cent piece the customer had given him. "There!" He threw the coins on the bed. "You'll get the other thirty cents when I have it—but I didn't steal your stupid candy bar. You've got a lot of nerve—"

"What's going on here?"

Charlie and Rachel both jumped. Neither of them had heard Grandpa Will come home. He stood in the doorway, looking at them with concern.

"Nothing." They said it together. "Nothing's going on."

"What was that about stealing, Charlie?"

Charlie looked down at his sneakers. "It wasn't important."

"Not important, Grandpa," Rachel echoed. "We were just having a little discussion."

Grandpa's anxious expression changed to a smile. He liked people to discuss their problems and settle them that way. He even taught a class in problem solving at Pike River High School, along with classes in history and civics.

"Well, that's all right, then. I'm going to the nursery to pick up a birdbath," he said. "Anybody want to ride along?"

"I have some phone calls to make," Rachel announced. "One of my committees, Grandpa. Otherwise I'd go with you."

"You shall be known by your good works," Grandpa teased. "How about you, Charlie? Want to come?"

"Sure." He liked doing things with his grandfather. "I'll be with you in a minute."

He waited till the door to the breezeway had closed.

Then he turned to his cousin. "Don't you ever say anything about stealing again," he said hotly. "I mean it! You'll be sorry if you do!"

"Threats!" Rachel tried to look indifferent, but her face was pale. She sat up, clutching a pillow in front of her as if it were a bulletproof vest. "I'll say anything I want," she said in a low voice. "And you'd better get me that thirty cents, Charlie Hocking. If you don't watch out, you'll turn into a *real* thief and spend five years in jail like your father!"

CHAPTER 2

Five years in jail. All the way across town, Rachel's smart-aleck warning repeated itself in Charlie's head. He tried not to listen, but the words seemed to follow him as he hurried after his grandfather, through the outdoor display behind the Garden of Eden Flower and Supply Store.

Beyond the tables full of blooming plants, crowds of painted gnomes and rabbits and herds of iron deer were ranged along the paths. Dozens of sassy yellow ducks made Charlie smile, briefly, just to look at them. Farther back, birdbaths were standing in rows.

"How about some ducks?" Charlie pretended it was a joke, but he meant it. He liked the ducks.

Grandpa strode on toward the birdbaths. "Your

grandmother would kill me," he called over his shoulder.

Charlie shook his head. Grown-ups were strange. After all, a person could make a birdbath by setting an old dishpan on top of a stool, but the ducks were really unusual. Someday, when he had a house and a yard of his own, he'd buy a whole family of yellow ducks and a couple of gnomes. Maybe a deer, too.

He bent to get a better look at one of the gnomes, then straightened quickly. The creased brown face reminded him of the old woman in the woods. The gnome's mouth was twisted in the same mocking grin. *I'll bet she's gobbling that candy bar right now,* he thought furiously. It was easier to be angry with the woman than to remember how she'd scared him.

"What do you think of this one?" Grandpa paused in front of the plainest, most ordinary birdbath of the lot. It didn't have a single flower carved on the base, and it was painted a dull gray.

Charlie shrugged. "The blue ones are nice."

Grandpa glanced at the bright blue plastic birdbaths. "Your grandma would kill me," he repeated.

Together they carried the gray birdbath to the checkout window, then loaded it into the trunk of the car.

"What in the world did I do for help before you came to Pike River?" Grandpa demanded. He sounded as if he really didn't know.

Charlie began to feel better. "We can set up the

birdbath when we get home," he suggested. "It won't be dark for a long time."

"Can't do it tonight." Grandpa Will swung the car into traffic and switched on the radio to get the five o'clock news. "The birds will have to wait one more day for their baths. This is Saturday, remember?"

Saturday. Cookout night. That's why Grandma Lou hadn't been home; she'd been doing some last-minute grocery shopping. Charlie's mood plummeted, but he tried not to let it show.

"We'll do it tomorrow, then," he said, and was silent the rest of the way home.

He and his father had arrived in Pike River on a Saturday, so they'd had to meet all the neighbors that very first night. Charlie had hated it. He was sure everyone gathered in his grandparents' backyard knew where John Hocking had been for the last five years. They must know, too, that Grandpa Will had arranged a job for his son as a maintenance man in the Pike River schools when he couldn't find work himself in Milwaukee.

Charlie's father hadn't seemed to worry about what other people knew. He'd moved easily from one group to another, shaking hands with the men and smiling at the ladies. *As if we belong here,* Charlie had thought bitterly.

Now, two cookouts later, Charlie knew the routine, but he wasn't any more comfortable. Saturday morning Mrs. Koch and Mrs. Michalski and Mrs. Drury and Mrs. Gessert would call to tell Grandma whether they would be coming to the cookout or not. Each family brought wieners or bratwurst for themselves and one dish for the group—baked beans or coleslaw or carrot-and-pineapple salad. Dessert was always the same—a big ring of fruit-filled pastry called kringle that Grandpa Will brought home from the Danish bakery. The food was terrific. If Charlie could have filled his plate and taken it indoors to the den-bedroom to eat by himself, he would have looked forward to Saturday night. But he had to stay in the backyard, watching his father and watching other people watch his father. He could hardly wait until nine-thirty when the neighbors packed up their baskets, folded their patio chairs, and went home.

His father wasn't like the other men, and that was the trouble. He bragged about how strong he was, and he talked about how hard he worked at the high school. The neighbors listened and nodded, but Charlie could tell they were bored. Mr. Gessert and Mr. Michalski were teachers, like Grandpa Will. Mr. Drury sold insurance, and Mr. Koch did something at the glove factory. They probably would have liked a chance to talk about their jobs, too.

His father called all the ladies by their first names, even though they were much older than he was and he hadn't seen them for years. Once he mentioned "my five years in the school of hard knocks." That was the worst time of all. Grandma Lou had turned away quickly when he said it, and Charlie had felt his own face grow hot. Even Grandpa Will had looked dismayed. His father hadn't noticed a thing.

Grandma and Rachel were preparing for the cookout when Charlie and Grandpa got home. His grandmother had cooked a kettle of chili—"for a change," she said—and the kitchen smelled marvelous.

"You don't have to set up chairs or carry stuff outside or anything," Rachel said as soon as Charlie came in. "I'm going to do it all." He knew she was apologizing for what she'd said earlier.

He went back to the car. He and Grandpa lifted the birdbath out of the trunk, and then they strolled around the yard, trying to decide where it should go.

"Did you and Rachel work out your problem?" Grandpa asked. He put a hand on Charlie's shoulder.

"I guess so. I don't know." Charlie didn't want to talk about it. He was still angry with Rachel. He'd thought they were pretty good friends until she'd made that remark about stealing. It changed things.

The quiet of the garden was pierced by a whistle. "Hey, look here! Look at what your old man bought, Charlie." John Hocking came around the side of the house carrying a battered guitar case. "I pawned mine when we were in Milwaukee," he explained to Grandpa Will. "Made up my mind I'd get a second-hand replacement with my first paycheck."

He was wide-shouldered, medium-tall, with

Grandma Lou's thick dark hair and Grandpa Will's light brown eyes. His face shone with excitement. Charlie felt a wave of resentment and disliked himself for it. *He acts like a kid,* he thought, and then, *So what? What's so terrible about acting like a kid?*

It was only terrible if you'd been hoping for another kind of father.

John opened the case, took out the guitar, and struck a pose. "What'll it be, folks? Gotta practice up before the company comes."

"I didn't know you could play the gee-tar," Grandpa joked. He sounded uneasy.

"Learned how two, three years ago," John said. "Believe me, I've had plenty of time to practice."

Charlie winced. Was his father going to tell the neighbors he'd spent his evenings in prison playing the guitar? "'Someone's in the kitchen with Dinah,'" he sang as he strummed. "'Someone's in the kitchen, I know...'"

There was applause from the the kitchen window, and they turned to see Grandma Lou and Rachel smiling at them. "We'll have some community singing tonight," Grandma called. "Good for you, Johnny."

John bowed. He even did a couple of soft-shoe steps. Charlie turned away. He'd die if his father did that in front of the neighbors.

As it turned out, the evening was much worse than anything Charlie could have imagined, and it had nothing to do with his father's guitar. Mrs. Koch started the trouble, halfway through supper, when she said, "Rachel, I hope you're going to try out for Sunbonnet Queen this Fourth of July. You'd make a lovely queen! I can just see you up on that float in the parade, and handing out prizes in the park—the way your grandmother did when she was your age. You look like she did then—same long dark hair and beautiful eyes."

Charlie nearly choked on a bite of bratwurst. The Sunbonnet Queen! He'd forgotten that part of his strange conversation with the old woman in the woods.

"I *am* going to run for queen," Rachel said calmly. "The winner has to be a good citizen of Pike River, and I've done lots and lots of things—" She blushed. "I mean, Grandma thinks I have a chance. . . ."

"Of course you do," Grandma Lou agreed. "You're a good citizen, if ever there was one, dear. All those cookies you baked for the Veterans Hospital, all those committees you work on, all the candy you've sold for the band."

"Charlie helped with the candy bars," Rachel said quickly. "He sold some this morning."

Charlie was still trying to remember what the old woman had said. He forgot for a moment that Rachel didn't believe there *was* an old woman. "You know the lady I told you about—the one who took the candy bar? She said she's the real Sunbonnet Queen. I didn't even know what she was talking about."

Rachel's blush deepened. "That's stupid," she

snapped. "The Sunbonnet Queen is always a girl—a *young* girl. You're just making up a story—and I know why."

"I am not." Charlie was starting to get angry again. First Rachel called him a thief, and now she was telling everyone he was a liar. "You know what she said? She said, 'Tell Will Hocking hello from the real Sunbonnet Queen.'"

"Why didn't you tell us before?" asked Grandma Lou.

"Because I forgot, that's why."

Rachel was close to tears. "You're making it all up because I didn't believe an old woman took the bar without paying for it—and I still don't believe it, so there! Now you're making fun of the contest, just to get even."

The Hockings and their guests looked from Rachel to Charlie, trying to decide what to make of this tempest.

"Now, children," Grandma Lou murmured.

"What old lady are you talking about, Charlie?" asked Grandpa Will.

Charlie groaned to himself. Now he'd done it. "Just a woman," he mumbled. "I was trying to sell her a candy bar, and she—she asked me if I was related to Will Hocking because I look like you. And she said to tell you 'the *real* Sunbonnet Queen says hello.'"

"He's lying!" Rachel sniffed. "I know he's lying. He ate that candy bar himself."

"I can't figure who'd say a thing like that, Charlie."

Grandpa was looking at him hard. "Where did you say she lives?"

"Outside town," Charlie said, wishing he had never started this. "There's that bridge over Pike River, and beyond that there's a woods." He paused, aware that they were all listening and watching him curiously. "I went back through the woods, and I saw this old house sitting by itself in the middle of a clearing. And I talked to the old woman who lives there. And that's all."

Mr. Michalski cleared his throat. "Sounds like the Delaney place. Some cousins inherited it from the old folks and rented it out for a while, but it's been abandoned for years. The cousins moved to Detroit, I think—never could sell it."

"Certainly an old lady wouldn't be living out there in the woods by herself, Charlie," Mrs. Koch said. "You must be mistaken, dear."

Charlie looked around the patio. It wasn't too dark to see the doubting expressions on every face. They all believed Rachel when she said he was making up a story. Every last one of them thought he was a liar.

It was Grandma Lou's reaction that hurt most. Her voice trembled when she spoke. "No one has been in the Delaney house for years," she said. "We all know that. You'd better stop this silly talk right now, Charlie. We don't want to hear any more of it."

Charlie jumped up and started toward the house. *He's John Hocking's boy, all right—making up a crazy story just to get attention.* That's what the neighbors were thinking, but it was much worse knowing his grandmother agreed with them.

"Come on back, Charlie," Grandpa Will called. "You haven't finished your supper. Let's forget the whole thing."

"I'm not hungry."

"Hey, kid, you can't leave now," John shouted. "You don't want to miss the singing, do you?"

The singing! His father hadn't even heard what was happening. All he cared about was his gee-tar.

"Yeah, I want to miss the singing," Charlie growled. He let the breezeway door slam, hard, behind him.

CHAPTER 3

Saturday night had been bad enough. Sunday morning was worse, with everyone except Rachel being super-polite to Charlie and not mentioning what had happened the night before. But it wasn't until Sunday afternoon that Charlie decided he had to leave Pike River.

He and Grandpa Will were out in the garden digging a shallow hole for the base of the birdbath. "We'll pick up a few flagstones later to set around it," Grandpa said. "That'll look spiffy." Then he changed the subject, so abruptly that Charlie knew he'd been waiting for the chance to say what he wanted to say.

"I took a few minutes to run out to the Delaney place this morning, Charlie. Thought I'd find out whether vagrants had broken in. Not that it's any of my business, I guess, but if it were my house I'd appreciate somebody checking once in a while. You never know when some member of the Delaney family might show up and try to sell it again, or even want to get it in shape to move in. Vagrants can wreck a place in a hurry." He was talking fast and didn't look up from his digging.

Charlie shifted the birdbath closer to the hole. "Did you see her?"

"No, I didn't. There wasn't anyone there, and frankly I don't think there's been anyone there for years. The front and back doors were locked up tight. I looked through the windows that were low enough, and I didn't see any sign of life."

"Maybe she was upstairs," Charlie said stubbornly. "Maybe she was taking a nap. Old ladies take naps."

"I don't think so." Grandpa Will picked up the birdbath and set it firmly in the hole. He stamped the earth around the base. "It didn't *feel* like anyone was there, Charlie. It felt like an empty house, and I believe that's what it is."

"Then you think I made up the old lady," Charlie said. "You think I ate that darned candy bar, the way Rachel said I did. Why don't you say so right out?"

His grandfather straightened up. "I think you're a fine boy," he said slowly. "I don't know what you saw, or what you think you saw. Maybe we aren't even talking about the same house, though I don't know what other one it could be. The point is"—he stepped back and looked Charlie squarely in the eye—"you have to be careful with the truth. You're old enough to know what's real and what's make-believe. Now, I don't know what the argument is between you and Rachel—"

"Sure you do," Charlie interrupted, and his voice cracked. "You're on her side. You believe her, not me."

His grandfather looked unhappy. "Rachel is your cousin and your friend," he said firmly. "We aren't against you, Charlie. But people are going to judge you on how you handle the facts. It's always better to—"

"I *told* you the facts! I went to that house, and I talked to the lady who lives there. She took a candy bar and she didn't pay me for it." He stomped on the loose dirt on his side of the birdbath. "Nobody would think I was lying if I was anybody else's kid."

"Now—wait—one—minute!" The words were spoken quietly, but Charlie knew Grandpa Will was furious. "Your father's a good man! Your grandmother and I are proud of him because he's paid for his mistake, and now he's ready to start over. He's enthusiastic, and he isn't afraid to work hard. You ought to be proud of him, too."

Charlie picked up a stone and pegged it across the yard. "He walked out on me," he said. "I mean, nobody made him hold up that store. If he hadn't done that, he wouldn't have gone to prison. I wouldn't have had to stay with Aunt Laura all that time."

"Now listen to me, young man!" Grandpa was

struggling to control his anger. "Your dad had a terrible time for a few years. First your mother died. Then he lost his job and couldn't keep up the payments on your house. And then he began drinking. . . ." Grandpa rubbed his chin. "I'm not making excuses for him, Charlie, I'm just telling you how it was. You hardly know him, I guess. You've been living together for a few months—that's not long enough to really know someone."

Charlie didn't want to hear *any* of this. He and Grandpa Will had become pals in the last two weeks. Charlie had even pretended, secretly, that Grandpa was his real father, and John Hocking was just someone who was living with them for a while. Now it was all spoiled.

Guitar chords floated from the den's open window, settling into a barely recognizable version of "The Battle Hymn of the Republic." Grandpa squeezed Charlie's shoulder. "We can talk again later, right?"

"Right," Charlie said, but he didn't mean it. He'd decided by then what he was going to do. He'd run away. He had money—fifty-seven dollars in his Model T car-bank the last time he'd counted. Fifty-seven dollars would take him a long way.

Where would he go? He'd thought first of returning to Milwaukee, to Aunt Laura, but he didn't really want to do that. Aunt Laura had tried to make him feel welcome, but Charlie had always known he was in the way. Besides, Aunt Laura's apartment was the first place where the family would look for him.

It would be better to go where no one knew him. California, maybe. He could mow lawns, or collect aluminum cans to make money, and if he didn't earn much, it wouldn't matter. He could live on the beach, catch fish to eat, look for rare shells every morning. Some kinds of shells were worth lots of money. He'd do all right in California, because there wouldn't be anyone to remind him that he was John Hocking's son and he'd better be careful how he handled facts.

But there was one piece of unfinished business he had to take care of first. A couple of nights later, with the sounds of his father's guitar as background, Charlie planned a return visit to the house in the woods. He had to go back. He had to prove to his family— especially to Grandpa Will—that he wasn't lying. He'd take the camera Aunt Laura had given him last Christmas, and he'd ask the old woman in the house to let him snap her picture. The memory of his grandfather's sharp words was as painful as a throbbing tooth.

The next morning, as Charlie walked along the edge of the highway, he pretended that this was the day he was leaving Pike River. This was the last time he'd cross the Pike River bridge, the last time he'd see all these pink and yellow and purple wildflowers blazing in the sun. Any minute now, a car would slow down to offer him a ride, and he'd be on his way.

He was thinking so hard that he almost bumped into the mailbox that marked the beginning of the road to the clearing. He looked at the side of the rusted box and made out the letters D E L on the bottom. Well, maybe Delaney was the name of the woman who was living in the house now. Maybe she was a daughter or a cousin of the original owners and had decided she wanted to stay here. Grandpa Will himself had said that the Delaneys might come back someday.

Charlie walked swiftly through the woods to the sunny open space beyond. The path to the front porch was longer than he remembered, and laced with prickly weeds. Empty windows stared at him as he approached. In spite of himself, Charlie thought of Grandpa's comment: *It felt like an empty house, and I believe that's what it is.*

He lifted the bulldog knocker, let it *thunk* against the door. There was no answer. He knocked again, with his fist this time, and then, astonished at his own boldness, he tried the knob. The door swung open, squeaking loudly.

The front and back doors were locked, Grandpa had said. Well, the front door was open now. Didn't that prove someone was here?

"Hello!"

Still no answer. Charlie wondered what to do next. He didn't have any right to be in the house—but what if the old lady was sick or had fallen and needed help? She was mean, and she said strange things, but he couldn't just walk away. Besides, if she were gone, he still wanted to find some proof that she'd been here a couple of days ago.

He moved into the shadowy living room. A couch

with cushions that sagged almost to the floor stood against one wall, and next to it was a lamp without a shade or light bulb. Beyond the living room was a dining room, empty except for built-in cupboards. He found himself walking on tiptoe, calling hello every few steps and holding his breath while he waited for an answer. The only sound he heard was the buzzing of a fly. It was terribly loud in the silent house.

A huge woodburning stove took up one wall of the kitchen. There were no pots or pans on the stove, and the scarred porcelain sink was empty. A cupboard door stood open a crack, and Charlie peeked inside, hoping to see a cereal box or a can of soup—anything that would suggest a person had lived in the house recently. But there was no food in any of the cupboards. In the last one there was a pile of newspapers, carelessly stacked. Something rustled behind them, and he closed the cupboard quickly.

The kitchen opened into a back hall with two closed doors. One of them led to another stairway to the second floor. Charlie opened the second door just a crack and blinked into a flood of sunshine. He was facing a glassed-in porch, its windows cracked and dirty, the bare pine floor streaked with grime. He pushed the door a little farther.

"GO AWAY!"

Charlie leaped backward, almost crashing into the opposite wall.

"I said, get out, boy! I haven't time for visitors!"

Heart thudding, Charlie reached again for the door-knob. She was there! She was living in the house. He was right, and everyone else was wrong.

Recklessly he pushed the door open and stepped out on the porch. The woman sat in a rocking chair at the far end, her dark head bent over folds of brown material. One hand moved rhythmically, making stitches in a hem.

Charlie cleared his throat. "I'm the boy with the candy bars," he said. "I was here last Saturday."

"I know who you are. Will Hocking's little brother." She didn't look up. Why wouldn't she look up? What was it about her that was different from the last time he'd come?

The woman moved her foot, and Charlie saw the candy bar lying on the floor.

"I came about the money," he said. "It's for the Middle School band. Remember?"

A blue jay flashed past the dusty windows. A floorboard creaked. Charlie wondered if she was just going to ignore him. Then she looked up, and he forgot all about the candy bar.

"I thought you'd be back," she said with a mocking smile. "Did you give Will my message, boy?"

Charlie stared unbelievingly. The woman's face was thinner than he remembered it. Her dark skin looked almost smooth, and now that she faced him he saw that most of the gray was gone from her hair. Loose dark waves hung about her face. Only her eyes were the same—and the mocking smile. She still seemed to look at him and through him at the same time.

"I said, did you give Will my message, boy?"

"He didn't believe me," Charlie said shakily. "He came out here to look around. He thinks I was lying because he didn't see you himself."

"He didn't come." The woman brushed her hair away from her face with an impatient gesture. "Some old man came looking around, but I don't want to see strangers." She scowled. "I told you to get out, too, didn't I? I'm busy. I have to get ready for the parade."

She didn't move from her chair, but there was a threat in her voice, a warning of danger. Charlie took a step backward. Then he remembered the camera in his shirt pocket. Aunt Laura had told him he must always ask permission before taking someone's picture, but the woman had returned to her sewing, as if she'd forgotten he was there. He aimed the camera hastily, snapped the shutter, and retreated into the hall.

The back door was on his right, down a short flight of stairs. Charlie hesitated, then decided he'd better leave the way he had come. If the back door proved to be locked, and the woman came after him, he'd have no place to run except to the basement.

He tiptoed through the house, looking over his shoulder at every other step. This time the front door stuck, and he almost panicked. But a second hard pull opened it, and he catapulted out onto the porch.

Sounds of summer—buzzes and hums and chirpings —rose around him. Nice, ordinary sounds. He leaped down the steps and ran all the way back to the highway.

Walking toward town, he tried to figure out what it was about the woman that had been so frightening. She had looked different, much younger than the last time, but that was more puzzling than scary. And she had just sat there in her rocking chair, hardly moving. It must have been the crazy, mixed-up things she said, and the way she said them. Especially, he decided, the way she said them. She was like—like a quiet mountain that could turn into a raging volcano at any minute.

And there was something else. Grandpa Will had said the house *felt* empty, and that was true. It had felt empty to Charlie, too, even while he and the woman were talking.

CHAPTER 4

FOURTH OF JULY SPECIAL!
RED, WHITE, AND BLUE CREPE PAPER!
GET READY FOR THE BIG PARADE!

The sign filled most of the drugstore window and was framed with shots of decorated bicycles, wagons, and doll carriages. Charlie studied the pictures, thinking the parade looked like fun. Corny, but fun. Too bad he'd be in California when this year's parade rolled down Main Street.

He took the film from his camera and handed it to the clerk. The drugstore was pleasantly dim, nothing like the huge, fluorescent-lit pharmacy near Aunt Laura's apartment in Milwaukee. But the high-school-girl clerk was like the clerks in the city. She acted as if she were doing Charlie a big favor by waiting on a kid.

"Tomorrow afternoon, late," she drawled when he asked how soon the prints would be ready. "If he gets to 'em tonight." She glanced toward the rear of the store, where the pharmacist was busy behind a high counter. "He develops 'em himself."

Charlie wanted the prints fast, so he could be on his way west. He walked home with dragging steps, thinking about the letter he'd leave behind. *Don't bother to look for me. I can take care of myself.* That sounded right. He'd mention the snapshot only casually. *I thought you'd like to see a picture of the woman in the old house in the woods. I went back and talked to her again. . . .*

Grandpa Will would feel terrible when he saw the picture. So would Grandma Lou and Rachel. They might show it to the neighbors at the next cookout, and then they'd all be sorry they hadn't believed Charlie when he was telling the absolute truth.

What would his father think? Charlie kicked a stone across the sidewalk. His father would be too busy playing his guitar even to read the note. . . . No, that wasn't fair. Actually, his father would probably be pretty upset. He'd never understand why Charlie had to leave Pike River.

The more he thought about the letter and the snapshot, the better he felt. By the time he reached home he had almost—but not quite—forgiven his family. Maybe someday he'd come back to Pike River for a visit, and they'd all tell him they were sorry they hadn't believed him.

Rachel and Grandma were sitting at the table in the breezeway. Grandma's typewriter was in front of her, and she was humming under her breath. Rachel was making notes on a pad of lined paper.

"Come help us, dear," Grandma said, as soon as she saw Charlie. "We're getting Rachel's application ready."

Charlie pulled out a chair and sat down. "Application for what?"

"For the Sunbonnet Queen contest, of course." Rachel eyed him warily. "The Fourth of July's just ten days off. But Charlie's not interested in this stuff, Grandma."

"Yes, he is." Grandma seemed determined to forget the argument at the cookout. "We're all going to be so proud if you're chosen, Rachel. Just listen to this, Charlie." She rolled a sheet of paper out of her typewriter. "'Rachel Devon is an outstanding young citizen of Pike River. She is president of her class at Pike River Middle School, and she works as the school librarian's helper one afternoon a week. Last December she made cookies and popcorn balls for the patients at the Veterans Hospital.'"

Charlie yawned, and Rachel stuck out her tongue at him.

"'Most recently,'" Grandma read on, ignoring them both, "'she has been selling candy bars so her school band can travel to Madison for a football game this fall.' "

"She's not the only one who's been doing that," Charlie muttered under his breath.

An eraser shot across the table and hit him on the forehead. "I knew you'd say that," Rachel snapped. "There's nothing wrong with getting other people to be good citizens, too, is there, Grandma? I'm just being a good influence."

"Good influence!" Charlie shook his head. "You get other people to do your work and you call that being a good influence?"

Rachel looked for something else to throw besides Grandpa Will's best ballpoint pen. "I sold one hundred and seven bars before you even came to Pike River, Charlie Hocking! You'd better stop—"

"That's enough. Both of you." Grandma looked dismayed. "Charlie, there's no reason why you shouldn't help with the candy bars if you want to. This isn't a contest to sell the most—the goal is to support the school band. And, Rachel, it *is* important that everything we list here is something you've done yourself. I wouldn't want you to make the mistake I did. . . ." She stopped. "Well, never mind that now. Water over the dam."

"Water over what dam?" Rachel demanded. "What mistake, Grandma?"

Grandma Lou sighed. "Doing this—helping you to fill out the application—makes me remember a very long time ago when I wanted to be the Sunbonnet Queen myself. My father was going to run for mayor of Pike River that year, and his campaign manager decided it would be a good idea if I entered the queen contest. If I won, you see, it would be good advance publicity before the campaign actually got under way that fall. The minute he suggested it, I knew I wanted to win more than anything in my life."

"And you did win!" Rachel exclaimed. "How did you do it, Grandma?"

"That was the trouble," Grandma said solemnly. "It was around the time of the Great Depression, and there were lots of people who couldn't find work. The Fourth of July planning committee decided the queen that year would be the girl who collected the most old clothes to send to the poor in Milwaukee and Madison. It was a fine idea, and lots of clothes were collected, but—it just wasn't fair."

"Why not?" Rachel wanted to know. "Collecting clothes sounds like a great idea."

Charlie could tell that Grandma Lou would rather not have told this story. "It wasn't fair because my father's campaign manager—that was Mr. Koch's father—went from house to house with me," she explained reluctantly. "At every stop he mentioned that I was Ira Swenson's daughter, and he implied that it would help my father's campaign if I won the contest. Later I found out that he had collected a lot of things himself and had added them to the stack we had stored in our barn."

"But that wasn't your fault," Charlie protested. "You didn't know he was doing it."

Grandma smiled at him. "That's right, I didn't, dear. Still, I felt terribly guilty when I found out, and it bothers me to this day—more than fifty years later. I enjoyed being the Sunbonnet Queen, but I would have enjoyed it more if I'd been sure I'd won the honor myself. That's why I want you to be careful, Rachel. If you do win, I don't want anything in the world to spoil it."

Charlie had a feeling there was more to the story than they had heard. He would have asked questions, but just then the front door opened and footsteps pounded through the house. His father appeared in the breezeway, his face an angry red.

"John, what's the matter?" Grandma Lou looked frightened. "You haven't been fighting, have you?"

"No, but I'd like to take a swing at somebody," John snapped. "That stupid Joe Adams, for starters. The nerve of that guy!"

"Who's Joe Adams?" Charlie asked. He'd never seen his father this angry before.

"My boss. So-called. Which means he should know more than I do, right? So this afternoon the paint is delivered for the high-school gym walls. I've been scraping off the old stuff for days, getting ready. I look at the paint, and it's the cheapest stuff on the market. Won't hold up for a year. And when I tell Joe that, he says it isn't any of our business. We don't do the buying and we don't do the complaining, he says.

We just do the painting. What do you think of that?" He looked around the table indignantly.

"Well, now," Grandma said. She put out a soothing hand, but John jerked his own hand away.

"I told him, if he wasn't going to do anything about it, I would. I'm going to call the president of the school board and tell him somebody's doing a lousy job. Probably letting the hardware store unload stuff on us that they couldn't get rid of any other way."

"You're going to call Frank Mason?" Grandma was shocked. "Oh, dear, you mustn't do that. Frank has a wicked temper, and if you talk to him when you're all upset—please wait till your father gets home. Talk it over with him."

"I don't need to talk to Dad," John exclaimed. "I know what to do." He slammed out of the breezeway and down the hall to the den.

For a minute no one spoke. Then, "Nobody's going to believe *him*," Charlie muttered. "He ought to know that."

Rachel gasped. "That's an awful thing to say, Charlie Hocking. I think Uncle John is brave."

"Since when?" Charlie retorted. "You never sounded like such a big fan of his before."

Grandma Lou pressed her hands together, almost as if she were praying. "The point is, he can't afford to take chances with his job," she said. "Oh, I wish your grandfather were here."

Charlie wished he were, too. Rachel had made him

feel like a traitor, but he couldn't help it. His father was a person who let his feelings get him into trouble; Aunt Laura had said so often enough. Now he was going to prove she was right again.

The voice in the den, fairly soft at first, was growing louder. Grandma Lou started to get up, then sank back in her chair. Rachel bent her head over her notes. Charlie stared out the window and wished he were already in California. He'd like to be walking on a white beach, splashing barefoot through waves that flattened themselves on the sand. He'd like to be anyplace but where he was, listening to the sharp click of the telephone being hung up. Listening to his father's steps, slower now, coming back down the hall.

"Is everything all right, John?" Grandma Lou asked uncertainly.

Charlie was shocked at the change in his father's face. All the angry color had faded, and he looked grayish, haggard.

"Not exactly all right," he said with a sick smile. "Mason told me I was wrong. He said the schools buy only top-quality materials. Can you believe that? I said I knew cheap paint when I saw it, and then— then I guess I got sort of excited and—"

White sand. Charlie concentrated hard. *Surfboards. Shells. A treasure map in a bottle.*

"So Mason said to forget the job. He said—this is an exact quote—'We don't need a hothead who blows his top every time he thinks he has a gripe.'"

"Oh, John." Grandma sounded ready to cry. "What will your father say? He worked so hard to get that job for you."

Charlie winced, and his father looked sicker.

"Mr. Mason is mean!" Rachel exclaimed. "Uncle John was trying to help. He was being a good citizen!"

John looked at Charlie, but Charlie turned away. He felt sorry for his father, but what good would it do to say so? After all, he'd brought this trouble on himself, by losing his temper at Mr. Mason.

"I think I'll take a little nap," Grandma Lou quavered. "I really am very tired."

She patted John's shoulder reassuringly as she left the breezeway, but her quick passage down the hall, and the way she shut her bedroom door behind her with a little slam, said she'd had enough of their troubles for a while.

CHAPTER 5

"Nobody's talking to anybody," Rachel complained. "Are you talking to me?" She stood in the den doorway, a clutch of papers in one hand.

Charlie shrugged, his eyes on the television screen. "Why not?" She was friendly one minute, rude and bossy the next, but it didn't matter. A week from now he probably wouldn't even remember what she looked like. "What's going on?"

"Uncle John's outside doing something to his guitar. Grandma's lying down again. Grandpa went out—I don't know where." She came in and sat primly at the other end of the sofa bed. "I just wanted to let you know that I didn't tell any lies on this application for the Sunbonnet Queen contest. Here's what I'm going to say: 'Her cousin Charlie Hocking helped to sell the candy bars.' Does that sound okay to you?"

"Why not?" Charlie repeated. She was a funny kid.

"So, will you help again tomorrow? Mr. Carly—
he's the band director—says we all have to sell a lot
more than we have so far."

Charlie considered asking why she'd want a liar
and a thief working for her, but he just didn't feel like
starting the argument all over again. "I don't know if
I'll have time," he said. "I've got a lot of stuff to take
care of."

"Like what?"

*Like packing. Like looking up a road map, so I can
pick the quickest route to California.* He wished she
would leave, but she didn't.

"Just stuff," he said gruffly.

"I'm sorry Uncle John lost his job."

Charlie nodded, still refusing to look at her. "I
don't want to talk about it."

"Well, you needn't bite my head off." Suddenly she
was her snappy self again. "*Nobody* wants to talk
about it. That was the longest, quietest dinner I ever
sat through."

"What's there to say?" Charlie muttered. "He
messed up—again. Period."

Rachel stood up at last. "You're weird, Charlie,"
she said. "You always sound mad when you talk about
Uncle John. At least he's here now, and you can talk
to him when you want to. You don't know when
you're well off."

Charlie was surprised. Rachel had seemed to him to

be perfectly contented living with Grandma and Grandpa in Pike River. He couldn't believe she envied *him*. Didn't she realize there was a big difference between having a father who was away being a missionary and a father who had been in prison? You didn't automatically think your father was great just because he was your father.

He opened his mouth to tell her he might have time to sell candy tomorrow, but she was already disappearing into her own room across the hall, her thin shoulders stiff with indignation.

By nine-thirty the troubled house was beginning to weigh on Charlie's nerves. Grandpa Will hadn't returned from wherever he'd gone, and Grandma and Rachel were in their bedrooms, their doors closed. Charlie switched off the television and wandered out to the patio.

His father lay on the lounge, the guitar case close by on the picnic table. He looked sort of small and sad lying there in the moonlight, but there was nothing sad about his greeting.

"Hiya, kid. Anything worth seeing on TV?"

Charlie sat on a picnic-table bench. "Nothing much," he said. "What are you doing?"

"Thinking." John sat up and swung his feet over the side of the lounge. "I've been making plans, Charlie —great plans. The more I think about it, the more I know it was a good thing I lost this job. I grabbed it too quickly in the first place. I can do better."

Charlie wondered if he could be hearing right. Had his father forgotten those painful months of job-hunting in Milwaukee?

"First thing tomorrow, I'm going to make a list of every store and factory in Pike River. Sales—that's where I should be. I think I'm a natural salesman. What do you say?"

"I don't know," Charlie muttered. "It's up to you, I guess."

"Of course it's up to me. If Frank Mason is too dumb—or maybe even too dishonest—to want to hear the truth, that's his problem. I'll get a sales job that pays a lot better, and you and I'll rent a place of our own. . . ." He was watching Charlie closely. "What's on your mind, Charlie-boy? You'd like your own room, wouldn't you? We can probably manage a TV in there, too."

"I'd rather stay here," Charlie said. "I'd rather stay with Grandma and Grandpa." *Or go to California and live on the beach.*

He expected a burst of anger, or else a pep talk about the fun they'd have in their own place, but instead his father leaned back on the lounge. After a minute or two he said, "I see," in an odd, flat voice. "Anything else you want to tell me?"

Charlie couldn't stop himself. "You shouldn't have yelled at Mr. Mason," he blurted. "You should have kept quiet. Now you might not be able to get another job. Not ever!"

In one swift movement John stood and picked up

the guitar case. Charlie got up, too, ready to duck out of reach if his father tried to hit him. They stared at each other, then John turned away.

"Nice to know my kid has so much confidence in me," he said over his shoulder. "That really helps."

Charlie sat on in the moonlight after his father had gone into the house. He didn't like himself very much, and yet he'd only said what he knew Grandpa and Grandma must be thinking. His father didn't think before he acted. He jumped right in, without wondering what might happen. Charlie had spoken the truth.

But telling the truth could be a tricky business. Charlie thought about the woman in the house in the woods, and how no one had believed him when he'd told about their meeting. He tried to imagine her right now, sitting on her back porch looking up at the moon. She couldn't really have grown younger, he told himself. It must have been a trick of the sun, or the different way she'd arranged her hair. What was the truth about *that*?

Grandpa's car turned in the driveway. Charlie considered going to the garage to meet him, but he didn't move. Grandpa's tall silhouette passed through the breezeway and into the kitchen.

"Hi, John." His voice carried clearly through the open kitchen window. Charlie realized his father must have been sitting in there alone. "Good news, boy. I saw Frank Mason—had a long talk with him. He's willing to take you back. He promised he'd look into what you said about the paint, too. If he finds out you're right, he'll reorder. But if he decides the paint is okay, you'll have to use it and quit complaining. What do you say?"

Charlie held his breath, waiting for his father to start telling Grandpa about the big sales job he was going to find tomorrow.

But when John spoke, Charlie hardly recognized his voice. "That'll be fine, Dad," he said. "Thanks for talking to Mason. I appreciate it."

Charlie heard Grandpa sigh, as he came over to the kitchen window and looked out.

"Things will be better tomorrow," he said. He seemed to be making a promise to John, and to Charlie, too, sitting there like a statue in the moonlight.

CHAPTER 6

The house was a small, pale-green cottage with marigolds blooming on either side of a winding front walk. The woman who answered Charlie's knock had bluish hair and brightly rouged cheeks. As soon as he started his sales talk she opened the screen door and motioned him inside.

"I adore chocolate!" she exclaimed. "Worse luck! I'd be better off if I never touched it. I'll take two bars—you just wait here while I get my purse."

Charlie waited gladly. He'd been going from door to door all morning, but it seemed as if the Middle School band members had already visited every house in town.

Laughter burst from the living room. "My card club," the woman explained, bustling back into the hall. "Here's two dollars, dear. Aren't you Lou Hocking's grandson?"

Charlie nodded. "Yes, ma'am."

"Well, when you get home you tell her Gert Schwanke said hello. And before you leave, trot into the living room there and see if any of the other ladies want to buy a candy bar." She seized his shoulder and propelled him through an archway. "Here's Lou Hocking's grandson," she announced, "come to sell us his marvelous chocolate bars."

The cardplayers turned to look at him, eyes bright with curiosity. *John Hocking's boy,* that's what they were all thinking.

"The money is for the Pike River Middle School band," he said quickly, so they wouldn't think he was trying to make money for himself. "A dollar a bar. There's almonds in them."

It turned out that most of the women had already bought from their grandchildren or from neighbors, but to Charlie's astonishment and delight five of the eight decided to buy again. "Just because it's such a good cause," one of them murmured, as she poked through her handbag for a dollar.

Her friends giggled. "You wouldn't think so much about the good cause if he was selling something else instead of candy," one teased. But then she bought a bar, too. Charlie hurried around the room, distributing candy and collecting money. Seven bars in one house! Wait till Rachel heard about this!

"Now you be sure to go down the block to Marie

Fisher's," Mrs. Schwanke said as she followed Charlie to the door. "She's at six twenty-one, and she's a dear little old thing—loves chocolate as much as I do."

Charlie felt great. Maybe Mrs. Fisher would be having a card party, too. He decided this would be his last call before he went home and reported his success to Rachel. After that, he'd go to the drugstore to see if his pictures had been developed.

Grandpa Will had been right: Today was a better day than yesterday had been. His father had gone off to work just as if last night's explosion hadn't happened. He'd been sort of quiet, had avoided looking at the others at the breakfast table—but the important thing, Charlie thought, was that he still had a job. Grandpa and Grandma talked more than usual, as if to fill in the silence.

Charlie was glad things were back to normal, because he didn't want to leave Pike River if his father didn't have a job. Now he was free to go. As soon as he had the snapshot of the woman in the old house, he'd write his letter to the family, fill his backpack, and be on his way.

He'd found some road maps in a drawer in the den and had discovered that Highway H, just west of Pike River, connected with 602. That was an interstate highway, and it would take him all the way to California. He hoped he'd get picked up by a truck driver or a tourist who was going straight to the coast.

Rachel had disappeared right after breakfast. When

he couldn't find her, Charlie had taken fifteen candy
bars from the box in the basement and had put them in
the canvas sack he'd carried before. Then he'd written
an IOU and left it on Rachel's bed. *I took fifteen bars.
Charles Hocking.* He didn't want her to come home
and start screaming that she'd been robbed.

He liked selling candy, or trying to. Walking along
the bumpy sidewalks, knocking on strangers' doors,
he felt more comfortable in Pike River than he did at
any other time. Unlike Mrs. Schwanke, most of the
people he met didn't know he was a Hocking. He
could pretend that he'd grown up here, that this was
the place where he belonged. And even when they did
recognize him, it didn't seem to matter. The women at
the card party had known he was John Hocking's son,
and now he had seven dollars added to the three he'd
collected earlier.

Mrs. Fisher's house was another small bungalow
set well back from the street. There was a driveway at
the side of the house, and there was a battered pickup
parked in the rear. The truck looked out of place, like
a tramp in a good neighborhood. Shades were drawn
across the front windows of the house, giving it an
unwelcoming look. Charlie decided to go to the rear
door.

As he reached the backyard, the screen door was
kicked open. A young man with longish brown hair
hurried out, his arms wrapped around a television set.
He put the television on the passenger seat of the

truck, before he noticed Charlie crossing the yard.

"Hey, kid! Don't go in there!"

Charlie hesitated at the steps. The man sounded tense. He took a step toward Charlie, his shoulders hunched.

"I wasn't going in," Charlie said. "I just want to talk to Mrs. Fisher."

"Well, you can't. She's sleeping—she doesn't want to be bothered."

"I wasn't going to bother her." Why was he getting so excited? "I just want to sell her some candy."

The man took another step toward him. "I told you, kid, she's sleeping. Now beat it!"

Reluctantly, Charlie retreated around the side of the house. He didn't understand what was happening here. If Mrs. Fisher was sleeping, what had the young man been doing in her house? If he was a television repairman, surely he couldn't just walk in and take the set. Suddenly Charlie had an answer, and it was a scary one. The man was stealing Mrs. Fisher's television set! Charlie had arrived just in time to catch him at it.

He thought of Tim Kelly, Aunt Laura's neighbor in the apartment building in Milwaukee. Tim had come home from work one evening to find his television, stereo, and camera gone. The thief had slipped in during the day and vanished without leaving a clue.

The old pickup clattered into motion. Charlie darted across the street and waited, looking from one house to another, pretending to decide which one he should call on next. When the truck backed out into the street, he turned his head just enough to see the license plate: AYK-175. He said it over to himself.

The truck turned the corner, and Charlie went back across the street. His heart pounded with excitement, but he wasn't sure what to do next. He could call the police and give them the license number, but he wasn't absolutely sure the man was a thief. A terrifying thought struck him. Maybe the fellow was more than a burglar. Maybe he was a murderer! Maybe he broke into Mrs. Fisher's house thinking no one was home, and she caught him in the act of taking her television set. She might be lying in there unconscious. Tied up! Bleeding to death!

Charlie went to the back of the house and looked at the door nervously. He'd have to go in and look. If he didn't do *something* quickly, and Mrs. Fisher was badly hurt, it would be his fault if she died.

He tiptoed up the steps and tried the door. It opened easily. Inside was a small, spotless kitchen and beyond that a hallway leading to the rest of the house.

Charlie stood in the middle of the kitchen. It was the second time in two days he'd entered a stranger's house uninvited. This second time he called an uneasy hello and received no answer.

The first door in the hallway stood slightly ajar. Charlie peeked inside and saw a vacuum cleaner, a broom, and a shelf full of cleaning supplies. He had started to close the door, when there was a rustle of footsteps in the hall. Before he could turn around, someone hit him hard between the shoulder blades and sent him hurtling into the closet. His head struck the shelf with such force that he barely heard the door slam behind him and a key turn in the lock.

He slid to the floor. His head throbbed, and when he touched his forehead he groaned with pain. As if from a great distance, he heard the whir of a telephone dial.

"Police—yes, that's who I want—this is Marie Fisher on Cutler Street. Six two one." The voice was quivering with fright. "You get over here right away —I've captured a burglar! He's locked in the closet— a great big fellow, mean as poison. I think he was going to kill me!"

CHAPTER 7

Charlie fingered the swelling on his forehead. The bump was getting larger and the pain was worse. When he shifted, the broom handle slipped from his shoulders and clattered against the door.

"You stop that! You can't get out of there, no matter how you try!" The quavery voice was just outside.

"I'm not trying to get out," Charlie muttered. He doubted he could even stand up. His chin rested on his knees, and every time he lifted his head another wave of pain washed over him. He discovered that the fingers of his left hand were sticky. *Blood!* He groaned. *I'm probably bleeding to death in here!* Then he sniffed his fingers and recognized the sharp, lemony fragrance of furniture polish.

Footsteps shuffled away from the closet door. "I'm going outside to wait for the police," the voice said. "If you do any damage, you'll just make it worse for yourself."

Dear-little-old-thing Mrs. Fisher, Charlie thought. He wondered how things could get any worse.

If it weren't for the very real pain, this could easily be a nightmare. Charlie's stomach lurched as he thought of Grandpa Will and Grandma Lou. What would they say if they could see him now, locked in a closet, waiting for the police to arrive? Like father, like son? No, they wouldn't *say* it, but they would have to think it. Everybody would.

Car brakes screeched, and there was a clatter of heavy feet entering the house.

"He's right in there," Mrs. Fisher announced. "And you'd better get your guns out before you open that door. I didn't see whether he was carryin' a gun or a knife. I just sneaked up behind him and pushed him into the closet."

"We'll take care of him," a deep voice assured her. "You just go out in the kitchen and wait, ma'am. Out of harm's way."

"Oh. Oh, yes!"

The closet door swung open. Charlie, doubled up on the floor, blinked at the light. The two policemen looking down at him appeared nine feet tall.

"Hey, now," one of them said softly, "will you look at that killer!"

Charlie struggled to his feet. "Not a killer," he said thickly. He groaned as one of the policemen pulled him out into the hall.

"What's your name, kid? What are you doing in Mrs. Fisher's house?"

"Charlie Hocking. Selling candy." Talking was dangerous. If he unlocked his jaws, he was afraid he was going to be sick all over the policeman's shining boots.

"You Will Hocking's grandson?"

Charlie nodded.

"John Hocking's boy," said the younger of the two men. "You know about him, Eddie."

Charlie's knees buckled. He started to slide to the floor, but the older policeman half-carried him down the hall and into the dim living room. He lowered Charlie into an overstuffed chair.

"Concussion, I bet," the young policeman commented. "That's some egg on his forehead."

Charlie leaned back. "I'm okay," he mumbled. "I just feel sort of—"

He was interrupted by the return of Mrs. Fisher; at least that was who Charlie supposed she was. A tiny, frail-looking old lady, she clutched a gray bathrobe around her and peered out at them from under a pink crocheted hairnet.

"So that's him!" she exclaimed. "Wicked-lookin', ain't he? I caught him red-handed, officers. He was just going into the closet—someone must have told him I keep my weddin' pearls and all the silverware in there. I just tiptoed up behind him and shoved." She demonstrated, nearly pushing the young policeman off his feet.

"Yes, ma'am." Both men looked at her solemnly. "You took a terrible chance, though."

"What was I supposed to do—let him take my silver? Not on your life!"

"I wasn't going to steal anything," Charlie protested. "I'm selling candy. Mrs. Schwanke said I should come here."

The older policeman looked interested. "What's Mrs. Schwanke got to do with this?"

"She lives down the block," Charlie explained. The headache was beginning to fade, just a little. "I went there first, and she said Mrs. Fisher liked chocolate so I should be sure to—"

"Ridiculous!" Mrs. Fisher snapped. "Gertrude Schwanke would never send a burglar to walk into my house and ransack my closet."

Charlie explained about the man he saw leaving with a television set. "He told me to beat it. He said Mrs. Fisher was sleeping and didn't want to be bothered. I figured he was making up a story because he was stealing the television."

"Stealin'!" Mrs. Fisher repeated. "Of course he wasn't stealin'! That was my nephew Jacob, and he's as honest as the day is long. He came over on his lunch hour to pick up the television and take it to a repair shop. I told him I'd be takin' a nap and he should just come in and get the set. I didn't sleep a wink last night—you may remember I called the police station twice to report Gregorsons' barking dog. Stealin', indeed! What a thing to say about Jacob!"

The older policeman held up his hand. "You say your name is Charlie Hocking, is that right? You're John's boy, and you're living with your grandpa and grandma now."

Charlie scowled. "So what?" he muttered. "My dad doesn't have anything to do with this."

"No need to get sassy," the policeman said mildly. "You say you came in here because—why?"

"Because I thought maybe that guy had knocked Mrs. Fisher out or tied her up. Or something." His suspicions sounded silly now. "He was in such a big hurry to get away. And I couldn't see why he'd be in the house if she really was sleeping."

"You should have called us if you thought something was wrong."

"I was going to," Charlie explained. "As soon as I was sure. I even got the truck license number—AYK-175. I thought if she was hurt"—he risked a glance at Mrs. Fisher, whose pink topknot trembled with outrage—"I'd better find her right away."

The policemen looked at each other. "Is that your nephew's license, ma'am?"

"How would I know?" Mrs. Fisher demanded. "You just quit askin' questions and put this boy in jail. Lou and Will Hocking are good people, but everyone knows that son of theirs went bad. And now here's the new generation headed the same way! If I hadn't locked him up for you, my pearls and silver would be long gone!"

The younger policeman went back to the closet and returned with Charlie's canvas bag.

"Whole bunch of chocolate bars in here," he reported. "All smashed up. He must have sat on 'em."

Charlie closed his eyes. Well, if Rachel wanted to make a big scene about the candy, she'd have to visit him in jail to do it.

The older policeman took Charlie's arm and urged him to his feet. "How do you feel now, kid? Still whoozy?"

"I'm okay." He wondered if they were going to make him wear handcuffs.

"Then if you'll check to make sure nothing's missing, ma'am," the policeman suggested to Mrs. Fisher.

"How could there be anything missin'?" she snapped. "I heard this burglar the minute he came into the house. Called out, he did, just to see if anyone was home. I had him locked in the closet before he could get into mischief. Now you put him in jail—otherwise he'll go right on breakin' into houses and stealin' from defenseless old ladies."

Charlie thought Mrs. Fisher was about as defenseless as a tiger. A small tiger, maybe, but a fierce one.

The younger policeman made a funny sound in his throat. "Well, as long as no harm was done—" he began.

"No harm!" Mrs. Fisher exclaimed. "What do you mean, no harm? He scared me half to death!"

"Yes, ma'am," the older policeman said, "and I'm pretty sure he's sorry he did that." He looked hard at Charlie. "Isn't that right, boy?"

Charlie nodded as vigorously as his sore head would allow. "Yes, sir. Yes, ma'am."

"Then we'll take you home. You better lie down for a while and put some ice on that bump."

"Well, I never!" Mrs. Fisher gasped. "You're goin' to take him home! After I went and captured him for you and everything."

"I know," the policeman said sympathetically. "But this boy is truly sorry for the trouble he's caused."

"I am," Charlie said, "honest."

For a moment they all just stood there. Then the policemen led the way though the kitchen to the back door, and Charlie followed. He was free!

The canvas bag in the backseat of the squad car reminded him of what he still had to face at home. The family would see the police car. They'd see the bump on his head. They'd smell the lemon oil. Rachel would count up the squashed candy bars. There was no way he could hide what had happened.

I should have gone to California yesterday, he thought. But it was too late for wishing. Even if he left tomorrow, he had to face his family one more time.

CHAPTER 8

"Marie Fisher did *what*?" Grandma Lou stared at Charlie. The hand that had been beating cake batter stopped in midair, and dollops of yellow batter plopped on the kitchen table.

"Grandma, the cake!" It was Rachel, of course, appearing like magic just when Charlie hoped she would stay away. "You look terrible, Charlie," she volunteered, "and you smell like lemon furniture polish."

Grandma pushed the mixing bowl aside and sank into a chair. "Be quiet, Rachel," she ordered. "Charlie, you tell me again what happened. I don't understand what you're talking about. Marie Fisher is a dear little old thing—wouldn't hurt a fly."

Charlie sighed. His head still throbbed, one

shoulder was getting stiff, and now he had to describe how he'd been taken prisoner by a tiny old lady who wouldn't hurt a fly. There was no way to escape. Grandma stared at him with something close to horror, and Rachel was obviously bursting with curiosity.

"I went into Mrs. Fisher's house to see if she was okay, and she pushed me into a closet and called the police. I landed on the candy bars—they're smashed." He said it fast, trying to get it over with. "I thought a guy was stealing her TV set, and she thought I was a burglar. The guy turned out to be her nephew."

Rachel snorted, and Grandma frowned at her. "It's not one bit funny," she scolded. "How anybody could think our Charlie was a burglar . . ."

"But Mrs. Fisher didn't know her burglar was our Charlie." Rachel chuckled. "You have to admit, Grandma, it's pretty funny to think of Charlie flying headfirst into that closet. And getting all doused with furniture polish."

"I don't have to admit anything of the kind!" Now Grandma sounded furious. "Instead of laughing, miss, you pack some ice in a plastic bag and put it on that poor forehead. Marie should be ashamed of herself, treating Charlie that way when he was trying to help. I'm going to call her this minute and tell her—"

"No!" Charlie exclaimed in alarm. "You'll make it worse, Grandma. She's already mad because the cops didn't arrest me."

Rachel handed Charlie a plastic bag filled with ice

and, in one of her quick changes of mood, set out to calm their grandmother. "Why don't you finish that cake, Grandma? Charlie loves cake. But no lemon frosting, right, Charlie?"

"Right," Charlie said grumpily. Rachel, teasing, was hard to take, but at least she wasn't making a fuss about the crushed candy bars. That was a surprise.

At first the ice made his head hurt more than ever. Later, though, lying in the den, he had to admit that the numbing cold helped. He'd taken a shower to get rid of the furniture polish, and Grandma had laid out fresh clothes for him to put on, just the way she did for Grandpa every morning. She'd told Rachel to bring extra pillows from the other bedrooms, and then they had both tiptoed away, leaving him to rest. The delicious smell of cake-in-the-oven drifted down the hall to the den.

After a while Charlie heard Grandpa's car turn into the driveway. There was an excited murmur of voices in the kitchen, and almost at once Grandpa peered into the den.

"You okay?" His kindly face was anxious.

"Fine. Honest."

"I think I'll just give the police station a call," Grandpa said. "I'd like to make sure they know this whole ridiculous affair was a mistake."

"You don't have to do that," Charlie protested. "I told them how it happened. They believed me."

"Well, they'd better!" Charlie was glad his grandfather hadn't been there to hear Mrs. Fisher. *Lou and*

Will Hocking are good people, but everyone knows that son of theirs went bad. And now here's the new generation headed the same way! The words stung more than the bump on his head.

He closed his eyes, and after a moment his grandfather tiptoed away. It was nice, Charlie thought, that his grandparents hadn't doubted his story even for a minute. Unexpected, too. They hadn't believed him when he told about meeting the old woman in the woods, but they were sure he was telling the truth about why he'd gone into Mrs. Fisher's house. Was it because they knew he wasn't a thief—or was it because they couldn't bear to believe anything *that* bad? He'd expected questions, but they had simply taken his word. At this very moment, Mrs. Fisher might be telling all her friends about Charlie Hocking the burglar, but there were at least two people in Pike River who believed she was wrong. Three, counting Rachel.

The only person who remained to be told about the day's adventure was his father. Charlie dreaded it. There would be an explosion, for sure. Charlie had talked Grandma out of calling Mrs. Fisher, and he'd convinced Grandpa there was no need to talk to the police, but he doubted that he'd be able to stop his father from getting involved. He'd probably call Mrs. Fisher, call the police, maybe even call Mrs. Schwanke to tell her she had a lot of nerve sending his son to a crazy woman's house. Charlie pulled a pillow over his sore head and tried not to think.

"What's the matter, kid? You have something against fresh air?"

The pillow slid to the floor and Charlie sat up. His father stood next to the couch, grinning down at him. The grin faded as he saw the bump on Charlie's forehead.

"What happened to you? And what does the other guy look like?"

"It wasn't a fight," Charlie said. "Didn't Grandpa and Grandma tell you?"

"Tell me what? Everybody's out in the backyard, I guess." His father sank into an armchair and stretched his legs. "You tell me," he suggested. "You sure it wasn't a fight?" He sounded sort of disappointed.

Charlie didn't know why, but suddenly he wanted to make his story as bad as possible. He *wanted* to get his father excited. "I went into somebody's house," he said. "The lady who lives there—her name is Mrs. Fisher—called the police. She thought I was going to rob her. Or maybe kill her." He waited. *Get it over with. Start yelling.*

"What were you doing in her house?" John asked. "Make sense, Charlie."

"I thought this man was stealing her TV set," he explained reluctantly, because he didn't want to sound as if he'd been trying to be a hero. "I thought he might have done something to her—it sounds crazy now, but that's what I thought."

"And she called the police?"

"After she sneaked up behind me and pushed me into a closet."

His father sat very still, looking at him. It wasn't the reaction Charlie had expected.

"Did she know who you were?"

"Not at first," Charlie said. "But when the police came, she found out." He took a deep breath. "They know about you. Mrs. Fisher said I was another generation going bad."

They know about you. Charlie realized it was the first time he'd ever referred directly to his father's past.

As far back as he could remember, Aunt Laura had warned him not to tell people his father was in prison. At first, when his friends asked, Charlie just said his dad was "away." Later he saw a television documentary about life on an oil rig in the Gulf of Mexico, and after that he'd told them that his father worked on a rig and didn't get back to the mainland for months at a time.

He'd been glad his father didn't want him to come to prison on visiting days. That made it easier to tell the oil-rig story—almost to believe it. He would imagine his father, very tall, tanned, big-muscled, and quiet, stopping work occasionally to stare out over the water and think about his boy up north in Milwaukee. It was a satisfying daydream that had disappeared abruptly the day John Hocking was released. The strong, tender father had vanished forever, and in his place there was a stocky, wisecracking stranger who gave Charlie a hug at the same time he was asking Aunt Laura if she still made the best lasagna in town. He'd filled the apartment with his boisterous laughter, had even made Aunt Laura giggle. Charlie had been miserable. He supposed he was angry with his father, for being gone for five years and for returning in this lighthearted way, as if five years in prison didn't matter. His father seemed to have forgotten the past. He didn't notice Charlie's anger.

Now six—no, seven months later—the truth opened up between them. *They know about you.* It was the same as saying *You're a bad person.*

His father stood up.

"Don't call anybody," Charlie said. "Please."

"I wasn't going to," his father replied. "It burns me though, that woman saying what she did. She had no reason." He grinned at Charlie, a tired grin. "You know," he said, "I never thought much about it, but I can see it isn't easy being John Hocking's kid." He hesitated. The grin vanished, then reappeared briefly. "Well, I'll tell you something else, Charlie. It ain't so easy being John Hocking either."

At five o'clock Charlie remembered the film that might or might not be waiting at the drugstore. He'd dozed for a while, and when he awoke the headache was almost gone. If he hurried, he could still get to the store before it closed.

He took his allowance—five dollars—from the top dresser drawer and went out to the kitchen.

"You shouldn't be up," Grandma said as soon as she saw him. But she watched approvingly while he ate a big piece of cake and drank a glass of milk. "I guess you'll do," she said, then started fretting all over again when he told her he had an errand he must take care of.

"Let Grandpa drive you in the car. He'll be glad to."

Charlie said he felt like walking.

"Rachel will go with you, then."

No, Charlie said, he'd rather go by himself. He finished his cake and hurried out of the house before Grandma could come up with more suggestions.

As he neared the drugstore, his excitement grew. For the last few hours he'd almost forgotten the woman in the old house, but now he could hardly wait to have proof that she really existed.

The same clerk was on duty in the front of the store. She was filing her fingernails and seemed annoyed when she had to stop to hunt through the box of completed prints. She examined every folder with deliberate slowness, until at last, when Charlie had given up hope, she took out one and tossed it on the counter.

"Guess that's what you're looking for." Her expression told him she didn't think *his* pictures would be very interesting.

Charlie paid her and hurried out into the late-afternoon sun. He tore open the envelope and thumbed through the prints.

There was a shot of his friend Terry Cutter holding up the baseball he'd caught at a Brewer game. There were three pictures of Pete Sternig's new Labrador puppy, and two of the automobile race Charlie had gone to with Pete and his father. There were several shots taken on the last day of school. Charlie was glad to have them all. When he lived in California, the pictures would help him remember his old friends.

He reached the last print and stopped in the middle of the sidewalk. *Maybe I do have a concussion after all,* he thought, as he looked again at the picture. *Something's wrong with my eyes.*

He went back to the first photo and turned each picture over, counting, until there was only one left— the picture he'd been depending on to prove he wasn't a liar.

It was a snapshot of a sunny glassed-in porch with dusty windows, an empty rocking chair, and a candy bar lying on the floor.

CHAPTER 9

The lights were on in the kitchen when Charlie reached home. He could see Grandma Lou moving from stove to counter and back again. At the other end of the house, a faint blue glow suggested his father and Grandpa Will were watching the evening news.

Charlie stood in the backyard and looked at the house. It had never seemed quite so inviting, and he had never felt so much a stranger. When he was gone, life would continue in there, and in Pike River, without him. Oh, they'd talk about him for a while—a boy who didn't always tell the truth, a boy who got in trouble with the police. His father's son. Even Grandma and Grandpa would be secretly relieved that they didn't have to worry about him anymore.

He walked around the garden looking at flower

beds, at the birdbath, trying to memorize details so he could recall them when he was far away.

"What's that—pictures?"

Charlie jumped. He'd been so busy feeling sorry for himself, he hadn't heard Rachel come outside. She was eyeing the packet of snapshots in his hand.

"Yeah—pictures." Charlie shoved the folder into his pocket.

"Show me?"

"It's too dark."

"In the house, silly. I like looking at snapshots."

Reluctantly Charlie followed her indoors and down the hall to her bedroom. Girls were a puzzle; at least, this one was: teasing, sharp-tongued one minute, warm and friendly the next. He wondered if they tried to be that way, or if it just happened.

"Come on, let's see them." Rachel sat on the edge of the bed and patted the space beside her.

Charlie hesitated. The biggest mystery of his life was in that folder. He couldn't show Rachel the shot of the empty rocking chair without explaining why he'd taken the picture, yet he didn't want to give her, or anyone else, a chance to call him a liar again. Maybe if he was very careful ... He took out the folder and removed eleven of the twelve prints, holding the packet high so Rachel couldn't see what he was doing.

"They're mostly guys I used to know," he said, "in Milwaukee."

Rachel went through the pictures, studying each

one. She lingered over the pictures of Pete Sternig and his puppy.

"Cute," she said softly. "I love dogs."

"His name is Rip. For Rip van Winkle. Because he falls asleep wherever he is."

"What are these cars?"

Charlie sat down and peered over her shoulder. "That was at a racetrack north of Milwaukee. There's Pete again, and there's his father. His dad is a great guy. He took us places—Brewer games, a Bucks game once. Pete's my best friend."

Rachel started through the pictures again. "These are neat," she said. "I never had a best friend before I came to Pike River. I have one now," she added hastily. "Jenny Chase. But she's in Colorado till August."

She paused. Charlie hoped she hadn't been counting the pictures as she looked at them.

"Why didn't you have a best friend before?" he asked hurriedly.

"We were always moving. We lived in Boston for a while, and then two different towns in Mexico. Then we went to St. Thomas, and for about six months we were in Puerto Rico. It was no use trying to make friends because I knew we wouldn't be around long. When my dad got his permanent assignment—in Zaire—my folks decided I should go to school in the United States. So I came here. And I've been here ever since."

She brushed a strand of hair back from her face. "I love Pike River," she said dreamily. "I wish I'd lived here all my life. There's a white house on Brooker Street that I call our house. I pretend my father is a minister here in Pike River, and I'm staying with Grandpa and Grandma for a little while because my bedroom in our own house is being redecorated. That's all make-believe, but I really am going to stay in Pike River the rest of my life. I'm going to know everybody, and everybody's going to know me—" She looked at Charlie sharply. "Don't you dare tell anybody what I said about the white house, Charlie Hocking. If you do, I'll—I'll push you in a closet and let you soak in lemon oil all night long!"

Charlie had to laugh. He was glad she'd told him about herself; now he understood why she was always so busy. It must be a full-time job, getting to know, and be known by, everybody in town. And he understood why being chosen the Fourth of July Sunbonnet Queen was so important to her. The Sunbonnet Queen became part of Pike River's history. She would truly belong.

"Where's the last picture?" Rachel demanded abruptly. Sure enough, she'd been counting. "Let me see it, Charlie."

Charlie made a quick decision. A few minutes ago he would have refused to take out the twelfth print, but that was before Rachel told him about her make-believe home on Brooker Street. She'd trusted him not to laugh. Maybe he could trust her, too.

He opened the folder. "Do you remember the cook-out when I told about the old woman in the woods?

And everybody said there wasn't any old woman? They said I was telling a whopper."

"No, they didn't," Rachel protested, "not exactly. They just said—"

"*You* thought I was lying, too," Charlie continued. "You said so. You said I ate that chocolate bar and made up the old lady. And Grandpa didn't believe me! He went out to the house the next day and looked around. He told me no one was there, and he was sure no one had been there for a long time."

"What's all that got to do with the other picture?" Rachel demanded. "Come *on*, Charlie."

He handed her the snapshot. "I went back to the house myself. I saw the woman again, and I took a picture of her. I wanted to prove to all of you that I was telling the truth." He leaned over Rachel's shoulder and pointed at the rocking chair. "She was sitting right there when I snapped the picture. I swear it! Her foot was next to the candy bar on the floor." He waited. "You going to call me a liar again?"

Rachel looked from the snapshot to Charlie and then back to the picture again, as if they were two parts of a peculiar puzzle. "Is this a joke?" she asked finally. "If it is, I don't get it."

"No joke," Charlie assured her. "The woman was sitting right there. We talked, and when I was leaving I took her picture. You're looking at it."

"But she isn't here," Rachel protested.

"She was."

Rachel's look of doubt changed to awe. "Then

you're lucky," she said slowly. "You're absolutely the luckiest person I know. I'd rather have seen her than —than be chosen Sunbonnet Queen."

Charlie blinked. "Why?"

"Because she's a ghost, dummy. A phantom! I've never seen a phantom in my whole life, and I don't know anyone else who has. Except you." Rachel held the picture up to the light. "She really isn't there. You can't take a picture of a ghost, you know. Not with an ordinary camera."

"Who says so?"

"I say so. I *know* so. Oh, Charlie," the know-it-all tone changed, "let me go out there with you next time. Please!"

Charlie shook his head. Rachel had just put his own worst suspicions into words. The woman wasn't real. He had talked to her twice, but *she wasn't real*. "I'm not going back to that house, ever," he said. "Why should I?"

"But you have to go back," Rachel insisted. "Don't you want to prove you were telling the truth about the old woman? I'll be your witness."

Charlie didn't like her assumption that people would believe her when they wouldn't believe him. He grabbed the snapshot and stuffed it back in the folder. "I don't care about that anymore," he said. "It doesn't matter."

Rachel groaned. "Come *on*!" she exclaimed. "How can you *not* want to find out the truth, Charlie? Besides, if we prove the house is haunted, everyone in

Pike River will know us. We'll be famous!"

"And you'll be chosen the Sunbonnet Queen for sure."

She ignored his sarcasm. "You'll be a hero, Charlie. People will be so sorry they didn't believe you in the first place. Especially Grandpa!"

Charlie sighed. That was another disturbing thing about girls; they could talk you into doing just about anything they wanted.

"Okay, we'll go back, once," he grumbled. "But if the woman isn't there, you have to swear never to tell anyone else about the picture. They'll just laugh."

"See?" Rachel grinned. "You do care." She jumped up from the bed and pulled Charlie to his feet. "I swear. Now let's make cocoa and write a list of what we'll need," she ordered. "Oh, Charlie, we're going ghost-hunting tomorrow morning!"

CHAPTER 10

Charlie was back in Mrs. Fisher's closet, only now the closet had shrunk to the height and depth of a coffin. He tried to call for help, but he couldn't make a sound. He heard a soft hissing. Mrs. Fisher was piping poison gas into the coffin.

"Sssst, Charlie."

He struggled out of the sheet that was tangled around him and sat up. His heart pounded. "Ssssst," the sound came again. Not poison gas after all. The door of the den opened a few inches and Rachel's dark head appeared. "Is it okay if I come in?"

Charlie glanced at the other half of the sofa bed. His father was gone, and the room was drenched with sunlight. "It's okay," he replied groggily, then discovered Rachel was already at the foot of the bed.

"What time is it?"

"Nine-thirty." Her tone suggested that he was the worst sleepyhead she'd ever known. "Grandma said we had to let you sleep. She said you needed time to recover from your terrible experience yesterday. All that lemon oil."

Charlie glared at her. "I'll bet Grandma never mentioned the lemon oil."

"What's the difference?" Rachel drawled. "The point is, do you?"

"Do I what?"

"Need more time to get over your terrible experience? Because if you don't, I think we should get started for the house in the woods right away. I've got the list."

Charlie looked at the paper she dropped on the bed. "Flashlight," he read aloud. "Candles. Skeleton keys. Sandwiches." He rubbed his eyes as if he couldn't believe what he saw. "If we go out there this morning, why do we need a flashlight and candles?"

"You had to search for the old lady last time, didn't you?" Rachel demanded. "Maybe this time she'll be in the basement, and we'll need lights to find her."

"If she's in the basement, she can stay in the basement," Charlie said firmly. "I'm not going down there to look for her. No way! And there's something I forgot to tell you last night. She wasn't an *old* lady the second time I saw her. Not as old as the first time, I mean. Her hair was different, and her face. And she was thinner."

Rachel stared at him in astonishment. "How could you possibly forget to tell me that?" she exclaimed. "Maybe it wasn't even the same ghost. Maybe it was the first ghost's daughter."

"It was the same—whatever," Charlie said. He returned to the list. "We won't need skeleton keys either. The front door will be unlocked, so we can walk right in, or else it'll be locked up tight the way it was when Grandpa came out there. If it's locked, we can forget the whole thing. We're not going to break in."

Rachel took back the list. "I've already made the sandwiches," she said coolly, "just in case you were going to say we don't need them either. I won't hike out there without taking lunch."

"Good idea," Charlie agreed. He discovered he was starving. That should convince Grandma he was over yesterday's terrible experience, even if the memory of it lingered in his dreams.

As they trudged along the highway outside of town, Charlie remembered something else he hadn't told Rachel. "The ghost was sewing when I took her picture," he said. "She told me she was busy getting ready for the Fourth of July parade."

"Really?" Rachel narrowed her eyes against the sun. "And the first time you saw her she said to tell Will Hocking hello from the real Sunbonnet Queen." Her voice rose excitedly. "Those are clues, Charlie! This ghost-person has come back from the dead because of something to do with the parade or with the

Sunbonnet Queen contest. If we can find out what the clues mean, we'll know what the ghost is doing in that house."

Charlie supposed she was right. The closer they came to their destination, however, the more he wished they'd stayed home. A ghost—this ghost, anyway—meant trouble. He didn't know how he knew, but he was sure of it. And now that Rachel believed his story about the woman in the old house, he didn't have to prove himself to anyone else. He could leave Pike River and let her tell people that they'd been wrong about Charlie Hocking. She was right; they *would* believe her, even if they hadn't believed him.

"Why don't you like your dad, Charlie?" The unexpected question blew away Charlie's thoughts about turning back.

"Who said I don't like him?" he retorted gruffly. "That's a dumb thing to say."

"No, it isn't. You always look angry when he talks. And when he plays his guitar, too."

"I don't!"

"You do. You don't say anything to him either. I'd talk to my folks all day long if they were here instead of in Africa."

She would, too, Charlie thought. She never knew when to be quiet.

"Is it because he was in prison? I *like* Uncle John. He's fun. Like a big kid."

"Yeah," Charlie muttered, "like a big kid." To his

relief, a familiar mailbox appeared on the edge of the highway ahead of them. "There it is," he pointed. "That's where we turn in. Let's eat the sandwiches first, okay?"

They settled in the grass next to the mailbox and opened the brown paper bag filled with peanut-butter sandwiches and pears. Rachel didn't say anything more about his father while they ate, or later while they walked through the woods, but she looked as if she were thinking hard. Charlie supposed she was lining up more nosy questions.

"There it is," he said loudly as they stepped out into the sunlit clearing. "Spooky, huh?"

"It *looks* haunted," Rachel commented. "It looks as if nobody could possibly be living there. I can't see why you even bothered to knock on the door that first time. I wouldn't have."

Charlie considered the dusty windows, the crooked shutters, the tangle of garden. She was right. What had made him approach the decaying old place? He didn't remember that it had looked so uncared for that first time.

"I guess I just thought I'd give it a try," he said. "Or maybe the ghost wanted me to come in. Maybe she wanted to talk to somebody from Pike River."

Rachel nodded as if this were a reasonable explanation. She pushed open the gate, and they made their way through the garden and up the steps to the front door.

Charlie lifted the bulldog knocker and let it drop.

Then he put a hand on the doorknob. "If it's locked, we leave," he reminded her. "No breaking in."

"Turn it," Rachel urged. "What are you waiting for?"

When the door swung open at his touch, Charlie didn't know whether he was glad or sorry. He led the way into the entrance hall and looked around, hoping the phantom wouldn't make him search for her again, room by room.

Rachel gripped his arm and pointed toward the back of the house. "The sun porch," she mouthed. "Let's go." She was very pale in the dim light of the hall.

A floorboard creaked sharply over their heads. Charlie whirled to face the stairs. "I've never heard that before," he whispered. "I bet she's up there."

"Then let's go up. We want to find her, don't we?"

They climbed the stairs side by side, stopping at each step to listen. The floorboards creaked again. Then Charlie heard a faint humming—breathless, delicate, and as frightening as any sound would be in a supposedly deserted house.

There's nothing to be scared of, he told himself wryly. *A ghost is humming, that's all.* He shot a sideways glance at Rachel.

"I hear it," she whispered, without taking her eyes away from the top of the stairs. "It's weird—like an echo from someplace else."

That was exactly what the humming sounded like. *Some other place, or some other time,* Charlie thought. The sound made him feel as if he were drifting backward through endless years.

They reached the upstairs hallway and faced a row of doors, all of them closed but one. That one was open just a crack; the opening was marked by a narrow band of sunlight across the hall floor.

Rachel knelt at the crack to peer inside, and Charlie peeked over her head. At first he could see no one, though the humming was louder. Then the graceful figure of a girl spun lightly across the room. She whirled, long black hair fanning out over her shoulders. Charlie leaned forward, trying to see the girl's face as she dipped and turned. This couldn't be the old woman, or even the middle-aged woman he'd talked to on the sun porch. And yet—she danced on tiptoes toward the door—yet it *was* the same person. She was no more than seventeen or eighteen now, and as lovely as a Gypsy princess. He couldn't mistake those glittering eyes.

"You said she was old," Rachel whispered. "She's not much older than we are, Charlie."

"She was old the last time I saw her," Charlie retorted. "Can I help it if she keeps changing!"

"She's so pretty! You never said—" Rachel shifted from one knee to the other and lost her balance. She fell heavily against Charlie, who stumbled backward against the opposite wall.

The humming stopped. For a moment there was silence, and then a shriek of rage that made Charlie gasp. Rachel collapsed on the floor, and the girl towered over them, her face contorted.

"What are *you* doing here?" she screamed. Charlie saw that she was glaring at Rachel, not at him. "How dare you come here? Don't you have any shame? Wicked! Wicked!"

Rachel gave a squawk of pure terror as the girl raised her arm. Charlie dragged his cousin to her feet.

"Get out!" the phantom screamed. "Get out of my house!" She took another step toward them, and Charlie and Rachel retreated, half-running, half-falling down the steps. The ghost-girl followed, arms outstretched. Her fury was like a wall pushing them downstairs, across the hall, and out the front door.

"Go away!" she screamed. "Oh, you're going to be sorry for what you've done. You'll be sorry for everything! I'll see to that!"

Charlie slammed the door behind them, and they raced down the porch steps and through the garden. He looked back only once, certain that if the ghost pursued them out of the house, he'd fall over and die of fright on the spot. But the heavy door remained shut, the windows blank and staring.

It looks like an empty house, he thought. *We're running away from an empty house,* and he ran faster than ever.

"Have to stop!" Rachel hiccuped. They dived into the shelter of the trees, gasping for breath. Charlie glanced at her, then looked away quickly, pretending not to see the tears that streaked her face.

"That—that girl—" she hiccuped again, "she hates

me!" Her voice shook. "Why should she hate *me*? What did I ever do to her?"

Charlie didn't know the answer, but he was sure his cousin was right. It was seeing Rachel that had set off that frenzy of rage.

"I think she's crazy!" Rachel exclaimed. "Really insane." She shuddered and walked on ahead along the narrow road. "Did you see the look in her eyes? She's not *normal*, Charlie!"

Charlie might have laughed, but his knees were still shaking, and he didn't want Rachel more upset than she was already. Still, it was pretty funny to talk about a phantom being normal or not normal.

"I don't see how a ghost can be insane," he said. "You're not changing your mind, are you? About whether she's a ghost or not?"

"Of course she's a ghost." They emerged onto the highway and stood for a minute watching a tractor crawling across a field. It was a peaceful sight, comforting to look at after what had just happened. "She's a ghost, all right. And not just because you say so, Charlie."

He waited, knowing there was more to come.

"Didn't you notice the floor?"

That superior tone again. "What do you mean?"

"The bedroom floor, silly. Where the ghost was. There she was, dancing and bowing and having a great time all by herself and *never leaving a single mark in the dust on the floor*. The dust was *thick*,

Charlie. And there wasn't one mark in it."

Charlie was impressed in spite of himself. Rachel made a good detective.

"And that's not all," she went on. "I'll tell you something that's just as weird. Remember the dress she was wearing?"

It was brown, Charlie recalled. Long. Like a pioneer girl might wear. It had a white collar and neat white cuffs.

"What about it?"

"The library has pictures of all the Sunbonnet Queens on display this month," Rachel said, "going back for years and years. And they're all wearing that same kind of dress. Long. A grayish or brownish color. Or maybe blue—I don't know. The older pictures are black and white. But every single one of them has a white collar and cuffs. Grandma says the Parade Committee has two or three of them in different sizes. It's the official Sunbonnet Queen costume, Charlie. And the ghost was wearing it!"

CHAPTER 11

"I can tell you're fretting about the Sunbonnet Queen contest," Grandma Lou said. "But you mustn't, Rachel dear. The committee never announces their choice till the day before the parade, so you might as well put it right out of your mind. Keep busy with something else."

"I'm not fretting," Rachel said, "and I don't feel like keeping busy, Grandma." She was slumped in a lawn chair, staring at the side of the garage. Charlie had been watching her ever since it became too dark to read his mystery. She looked dazed, he thought. She looked the same way he felt.

"Of course you're fretting," Grandma insisted. "I remember how I felt when I was a girl. I guess I didn't have to be concerned," she went on, and a shadow crossed her face. "I told you about all the help I was given. Still . . . Would you like to make some cookies, Rachel? Edie Koch gave me a recipe I want to try."

"No, thanks, Grandma." Rachel gave Charlie a desperate glance, but he didn't know how to help. The memory of the ghost-girl's furious attack, and the sound of her screams, had come between him and his book all afternoon.

The back door opened, and Grandpa Will and Charlie's father came out on the patio.

"Hi, kid." John tapped Charlie lightly on the head. "What's going on?"

"Nothing's going on," Grandma answered for him. "We've got two young people with everything to be happy about, and they sit here looking as if the world is about to end." A thought struck her. "Charlie, do you still have a headache? I think you should have stayed in bed this morning instead of traipsing off on a hike."

"I'm fine," Charlie told her.

"Well, then I'm sure I don't know what's wrong," Grandma said. "When I was your age—"

"How about a trip to the Chocolate Palace for some triple-dippers?" Grandpa suggested hurriedly. "My treat."

"Great idea!" John exclaimed. "I'm ready if everybody else is."

Grandma Lou said she was dieting and wanted to

stay away from temptation, but Charlie and Rachel
followed the two men out to the car. Grandma was
wrong, Charlie thought. He wasn't moping and he
wasn't sick. He was scared. Over and over again he
reviewed what had happened at the old house, looking
for an explanation. He longed to talk to Rachel, but
when he'd knocked on her bedroom door earlier in the
afternoon, she'd told him to please go away and leave
her alone. Since then, there had always been someone
else around.

Charlie's father talked all the way downtown. He
was still thinking about becoming a salesman, but
now he directed his enthusiasm at Grandpa.

"I'll apply in every town within fifty miles of
here," he said. "I'll have to buy a car, but then, I'll
have to do that anyway, once I find what I want."

Grandpa Will didn't say "Good for you!" but he
didn't say anything discouraging either. He even offered the use of his car for a few days. Charlie
squirmed, recalling his own response when his father
had tried to tell him about his job-hunting plans. *It's
just that he's always kidding himself about the great
things that are going to happen,* he thought. *And they
never do.*

The Chocolate Palace parking lot was crowded.
Swarms of insects danced around the overhead lights,
and a loudspeaker blared country-and-western music.
Grandpa took their orders and insisted on going to the
window for their ice cream himself. Charlie noticed

people calling out to him from other cars as he went up to the window—mostly high-school kids. You could tell how much they liked him.

Charlie's father noticed, too. "When I was a kid I was jealous of all the attention he gave other kids," he said thoughtfully. "Later on, I found out they were jealous of me." He seemed to be talking to himself, but Rachel, roused briefly from her gloom, smiled at him.

A car pulled in beside them, and John gave a little groan.

Rachel dug a sharp elbow into Charlie's ribs. "Here comes trouble," she whispered. "That's Mr. Mason— the one who fired Uncle John."

The big man started to get out of his car, but when he saw who was parked next to him he sank back. For a moment or two he stared straight ahead, then he opened the door again and stepped out.

"You'd better get Grandpa," Rachel whispered. "Mr. Mason looks as if he's still mad. I bet he didn't want to take Uncle John back, even if Grandpa's a good persuader."

Charlie was reaching for the door handle when his father suddenly leaned out of the front-seat window. "Hiya, Frank," he said, "how's it going?"

The big man hesitated. "Okay, I guess," he said finally. "How about you, Hocking?"

"Everything's terrific here."

Frank Mason looked over the top of their car. He

looked up at the floodlights. "About that paint," he growled.

Rachel squeezed Charlie's arm so hard it hurt.

"I have to tell you, I checked it out. You were right —inferior stuff—not what was ordered at all." Mason's heavy features reddened, as if he were working very hard. "You did us a favor by mentioning it, and I overreacted. I apologize. But next time don't check in at the top of your lungs, man. Don't act as if you're the only person in town who wants to do the right thing."

John Hocking opened the car door and jumped out. From the corner of his eye, Charlie saw his grandfather returning with a cardboard tray of ice-cream cones. He was walking fast, but his worried frown faded as John grabbed Frank Mason's hand and shook it vigorously.

"This is one heck of a relief to me!" John exclaimed. "Makes me feel a lot better, Frank."

"If he doesn't stop shaking Mr. Mason's hand, he's going to break it off," Charlie whispered.

Rachel giggled. It was good to hear her laugh again. "You're awful," she murmured. They watched as Grandpa set the tray on the hood of the car and joined in the handshaking.

"You should be proud of Uncle John," Rachel said, just as if she hadn't been as nervous as Charlie was a couple of minutes ago. "He didn't even say 'I told you so.'"

Charlie was proud, but he was uncomfortable, too. His own advice to his father kept resounding in his head. *You should have kept quiet.* He was glad Rachel didn't know about that.

On the ride home John gave a long, contented sigh. "I never thought that would happen," he said, grinning over the top of his triple-dip cone. "Frank Mason apologizing that way. Made me feel like ten million dollars."

Grandpa Will nodded. "I'm happy for you, son. Happy for Frank Mason, too. Saying he's sorry doesn't come easy to that man."

"The thing is," John went on, "I hate having somebody mad at me, even when I know I'm right. It's depressing—you know what I mean?"

In the backseat, Charlie looked quickly at Rachel. Her smile had vanished, and the dazed expression had returned. She was thinking about the phantom.

Oh, you're going to be sorry! the ghost-girl had shrieked. *You'll be sorry for everything!* Charlie remembered the tears that had streamed down his cousin's cheeks. She was hated by someone—and she didn't even know why.

"Well, now, folks," John said grandly, "I want all of you to know this has been a great little trip to the Chocolate Palace. You were around when I was down, so I'm glad you're here now."

Looking from his father's smile to his grandfather's look of amusement and satisfaction, Charlie felt a thousand miles away from them both. He'd been no help at all when his father was trying to do the right thing about the paint. Now he and Rachel had a problem of their own, and he didn't know the right thing to do about that either. He didn't even know where to begin.

CHAPTER 12

To his surprise, Charlie had a good time at the Saturday night cookout. The bratwurst, simmered in Mrs. Gessert's special barbecue sauce, had something to do with it. And Grandma Lou's baked-bean casserole was melt-in-your-mouth perfect. But more important than the food was the remarkable change in his father. John Hocking seemed relaxed, at ease. When Mr. Gessert told a long story about his freshman English class, John listened patiently. He laughed at the other men's jokes without trying to top them. The guitar lay on the patio step until Mrs. Michalski suggested it was time for a sing-along.

"Uncle John is happy," Rachel whispered. "I never saw him really happy before."

Charlie looked at her in amazement. He'd thought

his father was happy most of the time.

There was still another reason to enjoy this cookout night. Helping Grandma set up tables and carry out food had given him something to think about besides the ghost-girl. The experience in the old house had been on his mind constantly since yesterday, though he and Rachel had talked about it only once, when they'd met in the hall early in the morning.

"I feel awful," she'd whispered, barely moving her lips. "I had nightmares all night."

Charlie had had a nightmare, too.

"The whole thing is connected with the Sunbonnet Queen contest," she went on. "Oh, I wish I never entered the contest! I'd like to call someone on the committee and say I'm dropping out, but then I'd have to explain to Grandma Lou. And she'd never believe me if I told her why."

"Maybe she would," Charlie said. "Believe *you*, I mean. It's me people don't believe."

"No, she wouldn't! Not a chance! She really wants me to be queen, Charlie. It's important to her. If you really wanted me to do something, and I told you I wasn't even going to try because I'd seen a ghost— would you believe me?"

Charlie shrugged. "Maybe."

"You would not! You'd say I was making up a story because I'd changed my mind. And you'd be disappointed in me." Rachel's lips quivered at the thought of making Grandma Lou unhappy. "What can I do?"

"Well—we'll investigate, okay? Tomorrow."

"You mean go back to that house?" She looked sicker than before.

Fortunately, Grandpa had come along just then and asked for help weeding the garden "before company comes." Charlie didn't have the slightest idea of how they could investigate a ghost. He certainly didn't want to return to the house, any more than Rachel did.

Now, as his father started a last chorus of "Someone's in the Kitchen with Dinah," the phantom seemed far away. Charlie even sang a little, which he didn't usually do because his voice cracked when he least expected it.

"I think this has been one of the nicest Saturday evenings we've had," Mrs. Koch announced. "I'm sorry Merrill wasn't here to enjoy it."

Merrill was Mr. Koch. He was in Kansas City at a lodge convention, so Charlie and his father had helped to carry the Kochs' card table and chairs and Mrs. Koch's fruit salad to the picnic.

"Rachel and I'll take your things home," Charlie offered as the others began to gather their belongings. He was sorry to have the evening end.

Short, round Mrs. Koch reached up to pat his head. "I don't know what we did before you and your father got here, Charlie," she said. "I hope you stay with us for a long, long time."

Her kindness startled Charlie. He realized this was the first time all evening that he remembered he would be leaving Pike River soon for California.

They were cutting through backyards, with Mrs.

Koch and her flashlight leading the way, when Charlie had his bright idea. Maybe it had been there all the time, when he'd promised Rachel they would investigate the ghost. Maybe it was the real reason he'd offered to help Mrs. Koch. She knew all about the Sunbonnet Queen, didn't she? She even remembered when Grandma Lou was queen, more than fifty years ago.

He hurried to catch up to the bobbing flashlight. "You remember most of the Sunbonnet Queen contests, don't you, Mrs. Koch? I bet you know a lot of stories about them."

He heard Rachel's quick intake of breath.

"I do remember one sad thing that happened," Mrs. Koch mused. She shifted her empty salad bowl to the other arm while she fished in her pocket for the house key. "I don't know if I should tell you about it, though. Your grandma might not like it."

"Why not?" Charlie tried to sound unconcerned, but his heart was thumping a brisk tattoo.

"Because it happened the year she was queen," Mrs. Koch said, "and it was really dreadful. We never talked about it in front of her—just tried to forget it had happened." She opened the back door and led the way into her kitchen. "I don't think I should—"

The sentence ended in a bloodcurdling scream. Charlie stopped so suddenly that Rachel crashed into him. The card table and chairs they were carrying clattered against the counter.

"A mouse!" Mrs. Koch screamed. "I saw it when

the light went on. I saw it! It ran in there!" She pointed to the dining room. She was perched on top of the kitchen table, her feet drawn up under her. Charlie wondered how she'd gotten up there so fast.

"A mouse won't hurt you," Rachel said. She sounded as if she didn't approve of people who were afraid of mice.

Mrs. Koch rocked back and forth. "I can't stand them!" she wailed. Her glasses were askew, and there were tears in her eyes. "Oh, what am I going to do? Why isn't Merrill here!"

Charlie and Rachel exchanged glances. *Of all times!* his cousin's look said clearly. *Just when we were going to find out something. . . .*

"Have you any traps?" Charlie asked. "My aunt Laura had mice in her apartment in Milwaukee, and she set traps every week or so."

Mrs. Koch shuddered. "I suppose we have one somewhere. But if you think I can go to bed when there's a mouse running around my house . . ." She looked longingly at the back door, as if she wished there were some way to reach it without touching the floor. "I'll go over to the Gesserts'," she announced. "I can sleep on their couch. Merrill will be home tomorrow. He can set some traps then."

"You don't have to do that," Charlie said quickly. "We'll find the mouse—no problem. It's probably hiding under something. Where's your broom?"

Mrs. Koch pointed to a door. Charlie opened it and faced shelves of cleaning materials. The smell of lemon oil flooded the air. In spite of himself he stepped backward, and heard Rachel's not-quite-smothered snicker.

"Hurry *up*, Charlie!" she exclaimed. "Do you want the mouse to get away?"

Reluctantly, Charlie reached in and snatched a broom. With Rachel right behind him, he searched the dining room, looking under the table and chairs, sweeping under the heavy sideboard that filled one wall.

"Do you see it?" Mrs. Koch quavered from the kitchen.

"Not yet." Charlie decided it was hopeless. The dining room opened into a living room crammed with furniture. To the left was another door leading to a hallway and the bedrooms. The mouse could be anywhere in the house by now.

"Do something, Charlie," Rachel whispered fiercely. "I want to hear the rest of that story about the time Grandma was Sunbonnet Queen!"

Charlie gritted his teeth. "So do I! If you're so smart, *you* find the stupid mouse."

They moved into the living room, and Charlie swept the broom under the sofa, and the two armchairs, and the television console.

"What are you going to do if he comes running out?" Rachel asked. "Smack him with the broom?"

Charlie hadn't thought that far ahead. "Chase him out the back door," he suggested. "That's probably the way he came in."

"Right past Mrs. Koch? Oh, wow."

It occurred to him then that most of his problems involved elderly ladies. Mrs. Fisher. Mrs. Koch. Grandma Lou, once in a while. Old ladies might look harmless, but looks could be deceiving. Even the ghost-girl had been an old lady the first time he'd seen her. But *she* hadn't looked harmless at all.

They searched two bedrooms and the bathroom. The bedroom closet doors were closed, and Charlie said that meant the mouse couldn't be in either of them, though Rachel pointed out that the space beneath the doors was wide enough for a skinny mouse to slip through. Still huddled on the kitchen table, Mrs. Koch called out warnings to be careful.

"Any minute now she's going to decide to go to the Gesserts' for the night," Rachel groaned, "and that'll end our chance to find out what she knows about the contest."

"What's behind there?" Charlie pointed to a door at the end of the hall. It was opened a crack. Rachel ran down the hall to look, then returned to the kitchen, motioning Charlie to follow.

"I guess we found out where the mouse went," she announced cheerfully. "The basement door was open just a little, and he must have scooted right down there. I closed it, so you can forget about that old mouse until Mr. Koch gets home tomorrow."

"Are you sure?" Mrs. Koch looked doubtful.

"Oh, absolutely," Rachel insisted. "The basement would be the natural place for him to run to, wouldn't it? After all, the poor little thing was probably scared to death when we walked in and surprised him."

"Poor little thing, indeed!" Mrs. Koch lowered herself to the floor and straightened her glasses. "I'd rather find an elephant in my kitchen than a mouse."

Charlie grinned, but Rachel looked sympathetic. "Now you don't have to go over to the Gesserts' house after all," she soothed. "Why don't you just go in and lie on the sofa for a while, and I'll make you a nice cup of tea?"

She led the way into the living room and watched approvingly as Mrs. Koch lay down. "You go ahead and talk," she said. "Tell us all about when Grandma Lou was the Sunbonnet Queen. And talk loud, won't you? I don't want to miss a word."

She bustled back to the kitchen, and Mrs. Koch looked after her with a puzzled expression. "I didn't really promise to tell that story, did I? It was such a long time ago—I'm sorry I even mentioned it."

"I think you *should* tell us," Charlie told her, wondering what they were talking about. "It can't do any harm after fifty years, can it?"

Teakettle in hand, Rachel darted back to the living room. "Mrs. Koch, you have to tell us," she declared dramatically. "I'm running for Sunbonnet Queen, you know. Don't you think I should hear about all the problems that might come up? I mean, what if whatever-it-was should happen again?"

"Heaven forbid!" Mrs. Koch smiled wearily. "I can easily imagine you in the queen's costume, dear.

You'd be the very picture of your grandmother fifty years ago."

Charlie sat down in one of the overstuffed chairs. "Does she really look so much like Grandma did then?"

"She surely does. I've told you that before."

Charlie felt like a detective who has finally recognized a pretty obvious clue. "What about the other girls in Grandma's contest? Do you remember them, too?"

"Of course I do. That's what I was thinking about before—before the mouse! We always remember troublemakers, and if ever there was a troublemaker it was Katya Torin."

Rachel turned abruptly and returned to the kitchen. They heard the stove turn on with a little *pop,* and then she rushed back to the living room and settled expectantly in the other chair.

"Katya Torin," Charlie prompted, "who was she?"

"A strange, wild girl—I could *never* forget her." Mrs. Koch shivered. "She moved to Pike River one summer. Lived out in the country with her parents, but no one ever saw *them.* Just Katya. She came to school in September, though we never knew why. If she hadn't come, I doubt the authorities would have known the family was there. She certainly didn't come to learn—just sat there, scowling at the rest of us. Never talked. Never had a single friend, that I know of. And then the next summer she entered the Sunbonnet Queen contest, just as if she was—was like other girls. People laughed about it. . . ." A spasm of pain, or regret, crossed Mrs. Koch's face.

Charlie thought, *She was one of the people who laughed*.

"But how could she run for queen?" Rachel demanded. "I mean, if she never did anything but scowl? Grandma said all the contestants collected clothes for the poor that year. If Katya Torin did that, she must have talked to people."

Mrs. Koch adjusted the pillow under her head. "Well, I suppose she did talk, then," she said. "I know she went from house to house all over town asking for donations. And I guess folks felt sorry for her. Nobody thought she could win the contest, of course, but she looked so pathetic—so *needy*—like maybe she could use some of those old clothes herself. They gave her things, even when they'd already donated to someone else."

"To Grandma Lou," Charlie said.

Mrs. Koch nodded. "There were a couple of other girls in the contest, too, but we all took it for granted that Lou was going to win. Everybody but Katya. She just kept piling up clothes, and when the committee totaled the results, it turned out she'd brought in just about as much as Lou and the people who'd been helping her. It was a tie, you might say. So the committee had to pick the queen, and they chose Lou, since she was a native of Pike River and all. Everybody in town agreed they'd made the right choice, except Katya."

Rachel's expression was solemn. "I can guess how *she* felt."

Mrs. Koch shifted uneasily. "I'm not sure anyone even told Katya that Lou was to be queen—until Fourth of July morning, that is. Then all of a sudden there was Katya in the town square where the parade was getting organized. She was wearing a long dress —it might have been one she collected—and a sunbonnet she must have put together from cardboard. She went straight to the queen's float, just as if it belonged to her. When folks saw her coming, they tried to head her off, but it was too late."

"What happened then?" Charlie asked, not sure he really wanted to hear.

"She went kind of crazy, I guess. I was there—all of Lou's friends were there. Katya started screaming when she saw Lou up on the float, and then she began striking out at everyone around her. She screamed that she had a right to be queen—that she'd worked harder than anyone else. That was probably true, but still . . . She knocked down one girl, I remember. When she reached the float, she scrambled up and caught the hem of Lou's long dress. I'm sure she would have pulled Lou down if some of the men hadn't come running and dragged her away." Mrs. Koch wiped her eyes. "After all these years I can still hear her shrieks —the terrible things she said. They took her into the courthouse till she calmed down, and then someone drove her home. We never saw her again."

"You mean—" Rachel was wide-eyed. "You mean

she—did something to herself? Because she wasn't chosen queen?"

"I mean we didn't know what happened to her. Not then, anyway. The next day some of the committee members went out to the house where the Torins were staying. They were going to try to patch things up, but no one was around. The house seemed deserted. Katya didn't come back to school that fall, and the truant officer said the family had moved away. So we forgot about her—or we *tried* to."

Charlie leaned forward eagerly. "Is that all? Did you ever hear anything about her again?"

"Well, I heard something," Mrs. Koch admitted reluctantly. "A couple of years ago a nurse friend of mine—it was the same girl who was knocked down that morning in the square—she told me that Katya was in the mental hospital for the chronically insane in Madison. My friend saw her. She'd been there for years and years."

Charlie's head whirled. Rachel looked as horrified, and as confused, as he was. Could Katya Torin be the phantom in the old house? How was it possible, if the real Katya was a patient in a mental hospital in Madison?

"I wonder—" Charlie began.

He was interrupted by a breathless, barely smothered squeak from Rachel. She was staring at the sofa as though hypnotized. Charlie followed her gaze and saw two beady black eyes peering from under Mrs. Koch's pillow. Whiskers twitched around a pointed nose, just a couple of inches from Mrs. Koch's cheek.

"The tea!" Rachel rose from her chair like a puppet on strings. "Mrs. Koch, you have to come in the kitchen and show me where the cups are."

Mrs. Koch didn't move. "Look in the cupboard above the sink, dear. You can't miss them."

"No, please show me." Rachel tiptoed across the room and seized Mrs. Koch's hand. "Now, don't get up too fast," she warned. "Some people get dizzy if they get up too fast." *Do something,* she mouthed at Charlie, as she drew their bewildered hostess toward the kitchen.

Charlie picked up the broom. He moved swiftly down the hall, closing the bedroom and bathroom doors, opening the basement door wide. Then he rushed back to the living room and whipped the pillow off the couch. The terrified mouse took off toward the dining room. With a quick sweep of the broom Charlie sent it flying into the hall, then ran behind it all the way to the open door at the end. He closed the door, and was back in the living room when Rachel appeared with the tea tray. Mrs. Koch followed her carrying a plate of cookies.

Rachel looked at the couch, then at Charlie, who gave her a thumbs-up sign.

"This tea was a lovely idea," Mrs. Koch said. "So relaxing. You're good children, both of you."

Charlie smiled modestly. He was panting hard, but Mrs. Koch didn't notice.

"Now you can finish your story." Rachel helped herself to a cookie. "About what happened to poor Katya Torin."

"I think we've talked about that long enough," Mrs. Koch said. "Such a depressing business. Besides, there's nothing more to tell."

"Yes, there is," Rachel persisted. "Do you think Katya went insane just because she didn't win the contest?"

"I'm sure there were other much more important reasons for her breakdown," Mrs. Koch said primly. "She was an extremely odd girl to begin with. And there were rumors that her parents treated her badly."

"Where did she live?" Charlie asked. "When she was in Pike River, I mean."

"I never saw the house," Mrs. Koch replied. "I did think it might be the same one you told us about, Charlie, when you said an old lady stole a candy bar from you. It gave me a real start, your saying she sent a message to Will 'from the real Sunbonnet Queen.' But I knew there couldn't possibly be any connection with Katya Torin."

"Why not?" Charlie and Rachel asked together. "Maybe—"

But Mrs. Koch shook her head firmly. "No connection at all," she said. "Katya died in the mental hospital four months ago. My nurse friend sent me the obituary from the Madison paper." She set her teacup down with a clink. "And that's enough about that subject, I'm sure. You should be getting home—your family will be worried—and I must go to bed. Though I wonder if I'll be able to sleep, thinking about that mouse. I'm scared to death of 'em. If I ever got really close to one, I'd surely die!"

CHAPTER 13

They stood in a moonlit backyard halfway between Mrs. Koch's house and Grandpa Will's. A mosquito whined around Charlie's head, loud as a buzzsaw in the hot June night.

"I never believed in ghosts till now," Charlie complained. "I liked to *read* about them, but I never believed in them. I don't even *want* to believe in them."

Rachel didn't answer right away, and he had a weird feeling that she might no longer be there beside him. Then her fingers touched his wrist.

"You don't have to believe in just any ghost, but how can we *not* believe in Katya, Charlie? We've seen her. We've talked to her. You tried to take her picture. And now we know why she's here. She's the ghost of a poor lady who died in an insane asylum, and she's come back to Pike River to get even for a rotten thing that happened more than fifty years ago."

Charlie swatted at the mosquito. "Well, then, we'd better tell somebody," he muttered. "If she's going to try to—"

"She hates me because I look like Grandma Lou," Rachel went on, not listening. "She has the two of us mixed up. Losing the contest must have been the worst thing that ever happened to her. I want to be the queen myself, but I can't imagine caring *that* much."

Charlie surprised himself. "I can," he said. He felt a surge of admiration for strange, wild Katya. Without friends, without a family who cared about her, she'd tried to force Pike River to accept her as its queen. She must have known how hard it would be, but she'd tried, anyway.

"There's going to be trouble on the Fourth of July," Rachel continued. "I just know it. Whether I'm the queen or someone else is. And nobody's going to believe us if we try to warn them."

"Did you ever hear of a ghost that got younger?" Charlie asked. "That's the strangest part of the whole business. The first time I saw her she was as old as Grandma Lou. Next Saturday is the Fourth, and by then she could be just the age she was when—"

"When she tried to pull Grandma off the float." Rachel completed the sentence in a whisper. "Oh, boy!"

They started walking again, moving slowly through the buzzing dark. "We should tell someone," Charlie said again, but he knew Rachel was right. Who would believe them?

Grandma Lou had cocoa waiting when they reached the house. "We were about to send out a search party," she joked. "Now you just drink this down, and you'll sleep peacefully as babies all night."

Charlie doubted it would work, and it didn't. He was awake for what seemed like hours, turning and twisting. He thought about Mrs. Koch and the mouse, and about his father snoring gently beside him. Mostly he thought about Katya Torin. Every time he closed his eyes he saw her, looking down at them from the top of the stairs with hate-filled eyes. Who could sleep with a memory like that?

He didn't realize how restless he was till his father woke suddenly and switched on the bedside lamp. "For pete's sake, Charlie," he muttered, "what's the matter with you? Too much bratwurst and baked beans?"

"I'm okay. Just can't get to sleep."

John rolled over and squinted at him. "I don't suppose you want to tell your old man what the problem is." He waited. "Or is your old man the problem again?"

"I said I'm okay," Charlie muttered. "I'm sorry if I woke you up."

"No big deal." His father shrugged and turned off the light. "That was nice, wasn't it?" he said softly. "What Mrs. Koch said tonight."

"What do you mean?"

"About being glad you and I came to Pike River," John said. "About hoping we'd stay for a long time."

Charlie took a deep breath. "Oh, that."

"Yeah, that. What did you think I meant?" When Charlie didn't answer, he rolled over on his side, and in a few minutes he was snoring again.

Eventually Charlie slept, too, only to dream about the Fourth of July parade. He was standing on the curb in brilliant sunshine. Bands marched toward him. Floats, masses of red, white, and blue, loomed above him, and flags danced in the breeze. He was happy. After all, what could possibly go wrong at a Fourth of July parade?

Then he turned the other way and saw that as they passed him, the bands, the floats, and the flag-bearers were engulfed in boiling gray fog and disappeared completely.

CHAPTER 14

"Charlie! Get up and put some clothes on, dear. You have a visitor."

Grandma Lou sounded falsely cheerful and a little impatient. She'd sounded that way all week. Charlie supposed it was because she was so anxious to find out if Rachel would be chosen Sunbonnet Queen. More anxious than Rachel, he thought as he scrambled across the tangle of sheets his father had left. Since Mrs. Koch's revelations last Saturday night, Rachel hadn't even mentioned the contest.

"Charlie! Are you coming?"

"Right away." He pulled on cutoff jeans and a T-shirt and went down the hall to the kitchen. A man stood at the kitchen sink looking out over the patio.

He wore jeans and a blue work shirt, and there was something familiar about his nearly-shoulder-length brown hair.

"Well, here he is at last," Grandma announced. "Look who's come to see you, Charlie."

The visitor turned. It was Mrs. Fisher's nephew Jacob, the one who had been carrying off her television set.

"Hi, kid."

"Hi." Charlie stayed where he was in the doorway. "What's wrong?" He wondered if Jacob had just found out that Charlie had suspected him of being a thief and had come to beat him up. If so, there was going to be a massacre right here in the kitchen. Jacob Fisher was a lot older and at least fifty pounds heavier than Charlie. His shoulder muscles bulged under the blue shirt.

"Charlie," Grandma said reprovingly, "Jake has an invitation for you. There's no reason to look so hostile."

Jake Fisher laughed. "There's no reason why he should feel friendly toward me, Mrs. Hocking," he said. "If I hadn't been in such a hurry last week, maybe he wouldn't have gotten the wrong idea about what was going on. I was running late—my boss is a real bear if I take more than forty-five minutes for lunch—and I'd promised my aunt I'd get her TV set to the repair shop." He grinned at Charlie. "I'm sorry, kid. When I took the TV back last night, Aunt Marie told me what happened. I could see how it must have looked to you."

Charlie unclenched his fists. "That's okay," he said, "forget it."

"I'd be glad to," Jake said cheerfully, "but you don't know my aunt Marie. Now she's sorry, too. She asked me to pick you up this morning and deliver you to her house so she can apologize herself."

There were two houses Charlie never wanted to see again. One was Katya Torin's. The other was Mrs. Fisher's.

"She doesn't have to apologize," he protested, backing away again. "You tell her it's okay."

"She wants to talk to you herself." Jake glanced at his watch.

"I don't want to—" Charlie began, but his protest trailed off when he saw Grandma Lou's expression.

"Charlie," she scolded, "where are your manners? Marie Fisher is an old friend of mine. She may be a little prickly at times, but if she's ready to apologize to you, you must give her the chance. And have breakfast later," she added. Grandma hated to see anyone miss a meal.

Charlie gave up. He was trapped between the two of them, Grandma annoyed and pleading, Jake Fisher wanting to get this over with so he could go to work. He left the house with dragging feet, hardly hearing Grandma's promise to make pancakes when he returned.

Once they were in the truck and on their way, Jake relaxed. "Don't look so worried, Charlie," he teased, "My aunt doesn't bite. Not often, anyway. Say, do you like to swim?"

Charlie shrugged. "Don't know how."

"I won five medals in Central Wisconsin competition when I was in high school," Jake said, as casually as you could say a thing like that. "I teach a class of kids out at the lake on Saturday mornings." He glanced at Charlie. "You've got a good build for swimming. Interested?"

"I don't know if I'll be around," Charlie said. "I might—I might be away."

The pickup swung onto Cutler Street and then into the driveway at six two-one. Charlie shrank back against the seat.

"Well, you think about it, kid," Jake suggested. "You'll meet some guys your own age. Have a good time. We won't meet this Saturday because it's the Fourth, but next week . . ."

Charlie nodded and slid out of the truck. "Thanks for asking me," he said. "And thanks for the ride." All he wanted was to get this visit over with as quickly as possible.

Mrs. Fisher was in her kitchen when Charlie came up to the door. She let him in, looking tinier than ever in a crisp housedress and apron. There were cookies on a plate on the table, and a tall glass of milk.

"Sit down," she ordered. Her thick glasses flashed in the sunlight. "Eat."

Charlie sat, choosing a chair with its back to the hall closet where he'd been imprisoned. He thought Mrs. Fisher sounded cross, and not in the least apologetic. But when she sat opposite him at the table, he saw that her wrinkled cheeks were flushed a bright pink.

"Are you all right, boy?" she demanded. "Is the bump on your head givin' you trouble?"

"No, ma'am." Charlie bit into a cookie. It was double chocolate chip, his favorite kind in all the world. He took another one. Mrs. Fisher might be a tiger, but she could bake.

"My nephew Jacob is a good boy," she said in a voice that dared him to argue. "He says you made an honest mistake comin' in here the way you did. He says he might have done the same thing—might have thought there was monkey business goin' on—if he'd been in your shoes. Jacob says you did a brave thing, comin' in when you thought I might be in bad trouble."

Charlie didn't know how to answer, so he kept quiet.

"Have another cookie." Mrs. Fisher pushed the plate closer to him. Her handbag appeared as if by magic on the table, and she took out a checkbook. "How much are those candy bars you're sellin'?"

"One dollar." He hoped Rachel wouldn't object to a one-dollar check.

"I'll take fifty," Mrs. Fisher said, and her cheeks

became pinker than ever. "What do you say to that, boy?"

Charlie nearly choked on his cookie.

"I'll take 'em out to the Veterans Hospital for a Fourth of July treat," she explained, pushing the check across the table. "I go out to the hospital every Saturday—been doin' that for twenty-three years. You get the candy here this afternoon, you hear? It'll be a nice holiday surprise for my boys."

Charlie could hardly believe this was the same person he'd been hating for over a week. "I'll bring an extra bar for you," he said shyly. "No charge. Mrs. Schwanke told me you like chocolate."

"I do." Mrs. Fisher looked relieved now that she'd said what she had to say. She even smiled. "I do, indeed, boy. Have another cookie."

A half hour later he was home again, the check folded so that the tip stuck out of his shirt pocket. Rachel waited at the front door. She was very pale, and there were bluish circles under her eyes.

"Grandma's making pancakes for your breakfast," she reported. "What did Mrs. Fisher say? Did she apologize?"

"Not exactly," Charlie replied. He whipped the check from his pocket and waited to see her reaction.

It wasn't what he'd expected. "That's great," she said, almost listlessly. "That's really good, Charlie. Mr. Carly will be happy."

"How about you?" he demanded, irritated at her indifference. "Aren't you happy?"

"Sure I am. It's just that I have other things on my mind now." She followed Charlie into the kitchen, where Grandma Lou was pouring pancake batter into the skillet. When Grandma turned away from the stove, she was smiling so joyously that for a moment Charlie thought Mrs. Fisher must have telephoned ahead to announce her good deed.

"Isn't it marvelous news, Charlie?" Grandma exclaimed. "Aren't we proud of our girl?"

Charlie turned to Rachel for an explanation, and read the answer in her eyes before she spoke.

"I've won," his cousin said softly. "Mr. Cochran, the chairman of the Parade Committee, came while you were gone. I've been chosen the Sunbonnet Queen." Her lips trembled. "Great news, huh, Charlie? Just the best!"

CHAPTER 15

Charlie woke to the sound of firecrackers. He rolled over and looked out at a lead-colored sky.

"What do you say, sport?" His father sat up and yawned. "You ready for the big celebration? You've never seen a Pike River Fourth of July. They do it up right."

"Looks like rain," Charlie said. "Maybe they won't be able to have the parade."

His father poked him in the ribs. "Don't be so downbeat, Charlie. A little rain never hurt anything. Rachel will still be the queen, and Grandma and Grandpa will work the hotdog stand the way they did when I was a kid. And I'm going to win the guitar-playing contest. Rain or no rain."

Charlie was startled. "Win the guitar-playing contest?"

"Why not?" His father searched the closet for clean slacks and a sport shirt. "It won't do any harm to try. I guess I can fake it a little. Maybe there'll be a pretty lady judge who goes for short stocky guys that smile a lot."

Charlie got out of bed and stretched. It was just like his father to enter a contest he couldn't possibly win. Not that he was a terrible guitar player, but he certainly wasn't a very skilled one. Losing wouldn't bother him; he'd just laugh and say it had been a great experience.

"You going to be there, kid? Two-thirty—the band shell in the park. I could use a cheering section."

"I might be busy," Charlie said. "I promised Grandpa I'd help at the hotdog stand for a while." He had enough to worry about today without watching his father fall flat on his face in front of most of Pike River.

Grandpa and Grandma were already at the table when they entered the kitchen.

"Maybe Charlie knows," Grandma said, as they pulled up their chairs. "It's certainly beyond me what's going on in that child's head."

Grandpa Will winked at Charlie over his cereal spoon. "Your grandmother thinks Rachel isn't as pleased as she should be about being the Sunbonnet

Queen," he said. "You know any reason why that might be so?"

Charlie slouched in his chair. He couldn't explain what Rachel must be feeling today. He was still searching for something to say, aware that the family was watching him expectantly, when there was a step in the hallway.

Grandma gave a little gasp of delight. "Oh, my dear, come here and let us see you!"

Grandpa Will put down his spoon. "Well, well," he said, "if this doesn't bring back memories!"

Rachel came into the kitchen and walked slowly around the table. She was dressed in a long gown of soft brown material with a white collar and cuffs. Her sunbonnet was a lighter brown, and it had a white ruffle around the edge of the brim and a crisp white bow at the nape of the neck. Her hair fell in a rich coil over her shoulders.

Charlie thought she looked beautiful.

"Same outfit the queen wore when I was a kid," John commented. "You'd think they'd jazz it up a little. I mean, you look great, kid, but when I think of a queen I think of—well—"

"The Rose Queen in Pasadena?" Rachel smiled at her uncle. The blue shadows under her eyes were still visible beneath a fine dusting of powder. "This will always be the Sunbonnet Queen's costume, Uncle John. That's part of the tradition. Mr. Cochran came over yesterday afternoon and brought three brown dresses in different sizes. Grandma shortened this one just a little—otherwise it fit perfectly."

"I don't suppose it's the same dress I wore," Grandma mused. "Not after all these years. But it certainly looks the same. The Sunbonnet Queen represents the women who came across the country in covered wagons, John. She isn't supposed to look as if she's entering a beauty contest, for heaven's sake."

"Well, sure," John said agreeably. "Anyway, you look terrific, Rachel. Prettiest Sunbonnet Queen ever —I'll bet on it." He ducked his head, aware that he'd made another mistake. "Except for you, of course, Ma. You must have been the best of 'em all."

"Your mother looked exactly the way Rachel looks today," Grandpa Will said. "I never realized how much alike they are. Must be the costume, I guess."

Rachel shot a nervous glance at Charlie from under the deep brim of her bonnet. But when she spoke again, her voice was steady. "I have to leave right now," she said. "I'm supposed to be at the square early because the newspaper wants to take pictures while the parade is getting organized."

Grandma looked worried. "Breakfast first," she warned. "You can't stand up on that float for an hour or more without breakfast. You might faint!"

"I was up early," Rachel said. "I had cereal an hour ago."

"Then Grandpa will drive you to the square," Grandma said. "Or Uncle John."

But Rachel shook her head. "I'm going to take my bike," she said. "I don't need a ride."

"Your bike!" Grandma exclaimed. "You're going to ride your bike wearing that costume! You'll fall—and if you don't fall you'll probably get rained on. Look at that sky! Your costume will be all wet before the parade even begins."

Charlie had heard this kind of argument between his grandmother and his cousin before, but there was an extra edge in their voices today.

"I won't fall, Grandma," Rachel said firmly. "I never fall. I'll hitch up my skirt. And it's not going to rain until later. I listened to the forecast while I was getting dressed. It may not rain at all." She kissed Grandma Lou on the cheek, waved to the others, and drifted out of the dining room.

"Hey, I'll go with you," Charlie called after her. "We can walk—it's not so far." Grandma nodded vigorous approval.

"I don't want you to." The front door opened and closed. She was gone.

"You see!" Grandma said. "She's not her usual cheerful self at all. She wanted so much to be the Sunbonnet Queen, and now she acts as if she's only doing it because she has to. I just don't understand."

"Well." Grandpa looked puzzled, too. Then his face cleared. "The girl's nervous," he decided. "That's all it is. Riding on a float, presiding over the games in the park—that's a lot to think about. She'll be fine once the day gets under way."

"I hope so," Grandma said. "I wish we hadn't

promised to spend the *whole* day at the hotdog stand. I'd like to be with her when the parade begins. Let her know her family is behind her..."

"She knows that." Grandpa pushed back his chair. "Finish up, everybody, and let's get ready to go. We might as well ride to the park together, and then we can go our separate ways."

Charlie waited for the others at the back door. He wanted to get to the square as quickly as possible, but he had to do it without letting Grandma know he was worried. No matter what Rachel said, she needed him now. He was the only person in Pike River who knew about Katya Torin, and he wanted to be close to the queen in case there was trouble.

The streets and sidewalks were crowded with people on their way to the parade. Most of the children carried balloons or small United States flags. With the car windows open, the sounds of firecrackers and band music could be heard.

"That's probably the Middle School band," Grandpa commented. "They're playing the school song. They've got a lot of reasons to be grateful to you, Charlie."

John reached over and mussed Charlie's hair. "My son the salesman," he said. Charlie ducked away, pleased.

"I think we should just swing through the square and see how things are going," Grandma said. "I can't stop wondering . . ." She didn't finish the sentence, but Grandpa Will turned the car down a side street that led to the square.

They had gone a block when a motorcycle policeman motioned their car over to the side of the street. "You can't drive into the square, Mr. Hocking," he said. "We're turning back all traffic till the parade gets under way."

"We were just wondering about our granddaughter," Grandpa explained. "She's the Sunbonnet Queen this year, and her grandmother would like to make sure she got here okay and found where she's supposed to be."

"Saw her myself, Mrs. Hocking." The young officer peered in at Grandma Lou. "Just a few minutes back. She's up on her float and ready to go."

Grandma looked relieved. "Well, that's fine then," she said. "If you have a chance to talk to her, please tell her we'll be waiting for her in the park when the parade ends." The officer touched his cap and swung back onto his motorcycle.

"I'm going to get out here and watch the parade start," Charlie said. "I'll take some pictures."

"That's a wonderful idea, dear." Grandma beamed at him. "You tell Rachel to be sure to stay up on the float long enough for us to see her. Grandpa and I can take turns leaving the hotdog stand for a few minutes."

"Tell her she looks better than the Rose Queen ever did," his father shouted gaily.

"Right." Charlie hurried down the street before they could think of more messages. He was trying hard to stay cool, and yet the closer he came to the square, the more certain he was that he should never have let Rachel leave the house alone this morning.

The sidewalk became almost impassable. Charlie said hello to a half-dozen people who had bought his candy bars. "We've come to see your band in action," one customer told him. Charlie felt proud, even though he'd never heard the Pike River Middle School band perform himself.

The musicians, all looking hot and self-conscious in their purple-and-gold uniforms, were gathered on the corner when he reached the square. Beyond them a fire truck and a shiny red convertible were being maneuvered into line. The first float, a froth of white crepe paper topped by a big blue book, waited at the next corner. Red lettering on the book's cover urged everyone to READ ABOUT AMERICA. Around the sides of the float, boys and girls sat with open books on their laps.

Where was the Sunbonnet Queen's float? It would probably be close to the end of the parade, Charlie reasoned, since it was the most important. He edged his way through the crowd, looking for a brown dress and sunbonnet among the bright summer shirts and shorts.

"Hey there, Charlie. Don't forget next Saturday!" Jake Fisher leaned from the cab of his pickup to wave. The sides of the battered truck were fringed with short lengths of red, white, and blue crepe paper, and a roughly lettered sign announced I'D RATHER BE SWIMMING! The truck bed was filled to overflowing with boys in swimming trunks. One of them stood on a box in the center, arms extended, as if he were about to dive. While Charlie watched, the other boys pulled him down and a new "diver" scrambled into position.

Charlie waved back and hurried on. Behind him, the Middle School band began "The Stars and Stripes Forever." The parade was under way. He began to run, darting between couples and around families, until someone stepped squarely in his path and he had to stop.

"Charlie, dear, aren't you proud of your cousin?" It was Mrs. Koch, her round face shining. "I want to thank you for humoring an old lady last week," she chattered on. "I wouldn't have had a moment's rest if you and Rachel hadn't come to my rescue that night."

"That's okay." Charlie tried to sidestep around her, but Mrs. Koch wasn't ready to let him go. "I've already thanked Rachel," she said. "And guess what! We had our picture taken together this morning. We may be on the front page of the newspaper tomorrow —the Sunbonnet Queen and an old settler, or something like that."

Charlie stopped trying to escape. "You talked to Rachel? Just now?"

"Not much more than an hour ago," Mrs. Koch assured him. "She was here bright and early, and the paper took lots of pictures. She looks adorable in her costume."

An hour ago. She was all right an hour ago.

"Where is she now?" Charlie asked as casually as possible. "I want to shoot some pictures before the parade starts."

Mrs. Koch motioned toward the far side of the square. "Over there somewhere. You'll know the float when you see it, dear—a little log cabin on a hill. The queen always stands in the door of the cabin and waves to the crowd. As if she's waving to her pioneer family working in the fields, you see." Mrs. Koch looked pleased with that idea. "But you'll have to hurry if you want a picture before the parade leaves the square. I saw Rachel standing up there in the doorway while I was helping my Merrill with his lodge float. He's in the parade, too," she added proudly.

Charlie said good-bye and broke into a run. The town hall shut off his view of the other side of the square, but there were concrete paths cutting across the expanse of lawn and trees, and he followed one of these.

The parade was definitely moving now, floats and groups of marchers coming in off the side streets and settling into place. There were cheers and bursts of applause at each float. Charlie thought of his dream: bands, flags, floats—but no sunshine here, and no fog.

Maybe, he told himself, he was getting excited for nothing. Mrs. Koch had talked to Rachel, been photographed with her. She and the policeman had both seen her up on the float. If there had been a disturbance—if, for example, a dark-haired stranger had tried to drag Rachel off the float—Mrs. Koch would have known about it.

Charlie emerged from under the trees on the far side of the town hall just as another band began playing. The high-school musicians, dressed in red and black, were to his left. Charlie decided they didn't sound any better than *his* band, and their uniforms weren't as nice.

He threaded his way along the curb, and suddenly, right in front of him, he saw the little log cabin balanced on a hilltop. The hill was covered with a green-grass carpet, and there was an old-fashioned well halfway down the slope. In the doorway of the cabin the Sunbonnet Queen stood waving to her admirers. THE PIKE RIVER SUNBONNET QUEEN was lettered on a sign at the foot of the hill. Another sign proclaimed OUR OUTSTANDING TEENAGE CITIZEN.

Charlie realized he'd been holding his breath. He stepped back onto the sidewalk and followed the queen's float as it crept forward. It was all right, he told himself. Everything was all right.

The float picked up speed, and Charlie moved faster. Rachel knew what a queen should do, he thought. She was waving graciously, turning from side to side to greet her subjects.

But why didn't she raise her head and smile at people? The big sunbonnet hid her face completely. Charlie narrowed his eyes and stared at the slim figure. There was something else—something peculiar. Maybe it was the height of the float, but his cousin seemed taller than usual, more wide-shouldered.

He pushed through the crowds in front of him and dashed out into the street, ignoring the angry exclamations that followed him. He wanted to get to the front of the queen's float.

"What do you think you're doing?" a man's voice shouted angrily. "Get back on the sidewalk!" Charlie glanced over his shoulder and saw a policeman striding toward him. It was the younger of the two policemen who had answered the call to Mrs. Fisher's house; his expression said he recognized Charlie Hocking, troublemaker, and wasn't going to put up with any nonsense.

Hastily, Charlie raised his camera and pointed it almost straight up. He was so close to the front of the float that he could see under the brim of the sunbonnet.

"I said get back!" A hand grasped his shoulder roughly and pushed him away. "Stay out of the street!" the policeman ordered. "Take your pictures from the sidewalk like everybody else!"

Charlie leaned against a corner mailbox. "Wait," he gasped, but the policeman was already striding away.

There was nobody he could ask for help. Nobody who wouldn't think he was crazy if he tried to explain why he was more frightened at this minute than he'd ever been in his life. He could hardly take in the truth himself—that it had been Katya Torin, her child face transformed by triumph, who had smiled down at him from the doorway of the little log cabin.

CHAPTER 16

Once, years ago, Aunt Laura had taken Charlie to the beach, where he and another boy, a stranger, had run races. He remembered the way the soft sand clutched at their feet, slowing them down. He had the same feeling now; he couldn't run fast enough, no matter how he tried.

He had to find Grandpa Will; the shock of seeing Katya had blown every other thought from his mind. Grandpa would know what to do. He could stop the parade. Confront the phantom. Nothing could be done to help Rachel till he found Grandpa and—this was the maybe-impossible part—convinced him that there really was a Katya.

He broad-jumped over two little boys crouched on the sidewalk and passed Jake Fisher's truck. The swimmers were taking turns climbing onto the box in the center of the truck bed and pretending to dive off, to the cheers of the crowd. Up ahead, he saw the purple and gold of the Middle School band.

As he reached it, the parade halted. A rickety, overloaded truck had edged around the barriers, and now it was stalled in the middle of the intersection. Charlie pushed his way through the jeering crowd and darted across the street.

Beyond the band the sidewalk became a little less crowded. But even if he didn't follow the winding parade route, the park was a half-mile away. Charlie's heart sank at the thought. When he got there, he would have to find the hotdog stand. He'd have to talk to his grandfather without scaring Grandma into hysterics. It was all going to take *forever,* and he had a dreadful feeling that he had no time at all.

"Whoa, boy!" A hand grasped Charlie's sleeve and held on. He looked up and saw his father. "What's the rush, kid? You won't find a better place to watch the parade than right here."

Charlie blinked sweat from his eyes. His father wore a crazy straw hat with a red, white, and blue band. A bright red helium balloon was tied to his wrist.

"I don't want to watch the parade! I have to find Grandpa!"

A shadow passed across John's face and was gone. "He's at the hotdog stand way on the other side of the park. Busy as a pup with a new bone and loving it."

He studied Charlie's face. "What's wrong?"

"Rachel's gone!"

Charlie hadn't meant to say it. He was going to tell Grandpa, nobody else. The words had tumbled out by themselves.

"What do you mean, she's gone? Isn't she on her float?"

Charlie shook his head. "She's gone, I said! Someone else is on the float in her place!" He saw his father's look of disbelief.

"What are you talking about?" John demanded harshly.

"I saw her—a ghost!" Charlie choked on the word. There was no way to say it without sounding ridiculous. "Go ahead and laugh—I don't care! There *is* a ghost. Her name is Katya, and she's on the float in place of Rachel!"

John pushed his straw hat to the back of his head. "Aw, come on, Charlie. Make sense. Is this a joke? I like fun but—"

"It's not a joke!" Charlie tried without success to escape from his father's grasp. "I have to find Grandpa!"

"No, you don't. Whatever you were going to tell him, you can tell me. I mean it, Charlie."

"OKAY, THEN!" Charlie was close to tears. Seconds were flying by. He had to tell someone.

He began to talk. Katya Torin—how she kept changing, how she'd threatened Rachel—he raced through the strange things that had happened at the old house in the woods. Then he repeated what Mrs. Koch had told them about the long-ago contest when Grandma Lou had won and Katya had lost.

"Mrs. Koch says she died in an insane asylum just a few months ago," he finished breathlessly. "Now she's come back. You can believe it or not, but I know it's true. She still wants to be the Sunbonnet Queen, and this time she's done it. She's up there on the queen's float—*and I have to find Rachel!*"

John opened his mouth to say something, then closed it. He looked down the street. The purple and gold of the Middle School band still hadn't moved. "That's the wildest story I ever heard," he said finally.

"I knew you wouldn't believe me," Charlie muttered. "I knew that."

John mopped his forehead, and the red balloon bobbed foolishly. "Didn't say I don't believe you. But you have to admit, it's a pretty wild story." He frowned. "Could Rachel have gone out to that house by herself this morning? Is there any reason she'd do that?"

Something inside Charlie grew very still. He realized that this was what he'd been worrying about ever since he'd looked through the viewfinder of his camera and seen Katya. Rachel had been terrified when the ghost-girl drove them from the house, but she'd felt sorry for Katya, too. Was it possible that she'd decided to try to talk to Katya, maybe calm her down and avoid a painful scene like the one that had almost spoiled Grandma Lou's day as queen fifty-some years ago?

"Mrs. Koch said she had her picture taken with Rachel in the square," Charlie said uncertainly. "How could she be there and out at the house at the same time?"

"When was the picture taken? Just before the parade started moving?"

Charlie tried to recall exactly what Mrs Koch said. "Earlier. About an hour before. The newspaper took a whole bunch of shots. . . . But she told me she saw Rachel up on the float, too. And that policeman—"

"They saw *someone*," John said slowly, "just the way you did, Charlie. But between the picture-taking and the time when everyone was getting in their places for the parade, Rachel would have had about an hour to kill. She might have thought she'd have plenty of time to hop on her bike and go out to the house, make peace with Katya, and get back again."

"Only she didn't come back," Charlie groaned. "The phantom took her place." He could see that it was exactly the kind of thing Rachel would do. Being afraid would only make her more determined.

"So what are we waiting for?" John demanded. He loosened the string around his wrist and handed the balloon to a little boy sitting on the curb. "We'll use Dad's car—I have keys. It's right near the entrance to the park."

They were running down the street before Charlie

was fully aware that a miracle had happened. Someone believed him. Someone was going to help.

The trip out of town was agonizingly slow. Parade
goers had double-parked, making some streets impassable. Twice, they had to back up and look for
another route. Once a small girl erupted into the street
waving a flag. Charlie nearly hit the windshield, in
spite of the seat belt he was wearing.

"Sorry about that." His father kept glancing sideways at Charlie, his eyes full of questions.

"Why did you go to that house in the first place? I
don't get it. And why did you go back?"

"I wanted to sell more candy bars than anyone
else," Charlie said. "It was just one more place to try.
And the house didn't look so bad the first time I saw
it—I mean, it looked the same as it does now, I guess,
but I just didn't notice. She—Katya—opened the
door right away. She said I reminded her of someone,
and it turned out to be Grandpa Will. I guess I look
the way he did when he was a kid—the way Rachel
looks like Grandma. And Katya liked him."

John nodded. "I suppose *everybody* liked him when
he was a kid, same as they do now." John sounded
wistful, as if Grandpa's popularity made him a little
sad. Charlie guessed it must be hard being the son of
the best-liked man in town, if you weren't anything
like him.

"I went back the second time," Charlie explained,
"because nobody believed me about the first time.

Katya stole a chocolate bar from me, and Rachel said I must have eaten it myself. And Grandpa said there was no one living in the house. I wanted to take a picture of the old lady to prove she was there." He hesitated. "She was a lot younger by then."

"Where's the picture?"

"She wasn't in it. Just the chair she was sitting in."

John rolled his eyes. "Mysteriouser and mysteriouser," he muttered.

They crossed the Pike River bridge and left the town behind them. "You'd better slow down now," Charlie warned, "the road through the woods is right —there!" He pointed at the sagging mailbox.

John guided the car into the narrow lane. It was always dark under the trees, and today's overcast sky had turned the road into a tunnel.

"Maybe we're wrong about Rachel coming out here," John said doubtfully. "I don't think *I'd* come in on my bike, all alone. Especially if I thought there was a ghost waiting down the road."

Charlie clenched his fists. Rachel would. He was sure of it. Besides, where else was there to look?

The car struggled out of the rutted lane and into the clearing. John stopped close to the gate and switched off the lights.

"Good lord, no!"

"It's so foggy," Charlie said. "Why—"

But his father was already out of the car. "That's not fog, it's smoke!" he shouted. "Look at the house!"

Charlie looked. Red-orange flames leaped behind a

living-room window. Smoke curls wreathed the window frames and the front door.

"You go for help, Charlie! Stop a car out on the highway and tell them to call the fire department! I'm going around to the back and look for a way in."

Charlie couldn't move. As he stared in horror at the house, a window exploded from the heat. The flames danced higher.

His father was running along the side of the house. Charlie raced after him. Before he reached the backyard he heard the sound of more breaking glass, and he turned the corner in time to see John disappearing through the shattered window. The back door must be locked. Glass littered the ground, and puffs of smoke drifted from the window.

"Wait for me!" Charlie shouted. He climbed up on the wooden crate his father had used to enter. A ragged curtain blew in the hot wind, and he used it to pull himself up and over the sill.

He was in the back hall, facing the smoke-filled kitchen. From the front of the house came an ominous crackling. He couldn't see his father.

"Dad!" Charlie dropped to his knees, struggling for breath. Footsteps clattered across the kitchen, and his father appeared through the smoke. He was red-faced, coughing.

"I told you to go for help, Charlie! Now beat it!"

"I'm going with you," Charlie gasped. "We have to find Rachel!" *And I don't want to leave you here!*

"No!" John looked angry and scared. "If she's here,

I'll find her. I don't have time to argue with you—the house is going to be one big bonfire in a few minutes. Go, Charlie!"

Charlie crawled backward toward the window. If only he'd never seen this place, never tried to sell those stupid candy bars! Who cared whether the Middle School band went to Madison next fall? From the first day this house had brought him nothing but trouble—and now it was going to kill the people he loved.

"Hey, Rachel!" he shouted desperately. "Rachel, are you in here?"

From somewhere far off—upstairs—came a thud and a faint scream.

"That's it!" John turned and started back toward the front of the house. He was halfway across the dining room when there was a terrifying *crack,* and a beam fell in front of him. He staggered back, arms raised to protect his face from a wall of flame.

"Dad, there's another stairway!" Charlie threw open the nearest door, revealing the narrow staircase he'd seen on his second visit to the house.

John crouched low and raced up the steps, two at a time. At the top he turned and looked down at Charlie.

"Get *out,* kid!" he roared. "Fire department!" Then he was gone.

Charlie climbed over the sill of the broken window and dropped heavily to the crate below. As he ran around the side of the house, he could feel heat from inside the walls, an ugly pulsing like the beat of a huge heart. It was the worst sound he'd ever heard.

A gleam of metal caught his eye as he dashed across the clearing. Rachel's bicycle, half-hidden by underbrush, leaned against a tree. He dragged it to the road, and a moment later he was flying toward the highway.

It was a rough ride. The ruts were deep, and he kept bouncing in and out of them. When the road ended at last, he wasn't ready, and he catapulted out onto the highway. Brakes screeched as a truck swerved to miss him.

Charlie shouted, but the bearded driver was already out of his cab.

"You crazy kid! Why don't you look where you're going? Don't you know enough to—" Charlie's expression cut off the scolding. "You in trouble?"

He listened, combing his beard with his fingers, while Charlie told him about the fire. "I know the place," he said. "Probably some tramp moved in, built a fire to heat food. You say your dad's back there? Not in the house, I hope."

Charlie looked away. "He said to get the fire department!"

"I'll do that." The man climbed back into his truck. "At least, I'll try. But that old firetrap will be long gone when the trucks get out here. They're in the parade, you know—it'll take time to round 'em up. You want to drive into town with me?"

Charlie shook his head. He turned the bike back

toward the wooded road, and the truck pulled away. Briefly, he watched it go, wishing the man would drive faster. Much faster! He felt as if he were caught in a time warp, where everything moved slowly except the fire. The fire would be racing through the house, eating it up. *A bonfire,* his father had said.

The smell of smoke filled his nostrils and started him coughing before he reached the clearing. As he burst out of the woods, a scorching wind blew across the garden. Hot, dry air blinded him for a moment, but not before he saw that the house had become an inferno. The walls still stood, but every window framed a curtain of fire. Orange tongues licked at the eaves.

"Dad! Rachel!" Charlie started to run toward the burning shell, but another blast of hot wind drove him back. There was nothing he or anyone could do. He stumbled against the fence and clung there, coughing and crying.

When he looked up again, his father and Rachel were coming toward him through the smoke.

Ghosts, he thought, *I'm seeing ghosts again.* He closed his eyes, and opened them quickly. The two figures were still there.

Their scared, soot-stained faces looked wonderfully real.

CHAPTER 17

Thunder growled, barely heard above the crackling of the fire. Charlie crouched in tall grass between his father and Rachel, looking from one to the other. His father's shirt was torn; he held his left arm carefully against his chest. Rachel sat cross-legged, her long brown gown spread around her. The sunbonnet in her lap had a crease in its brim, and the ruffle was grimy. Except for that, and the soot on her cheeks and nose, she looked almost untouched by whatever it was that had happened to her.

"Uncle John hurt his arm breaking down the closet door," she told Charlie. "He saved my life!" Her tone said more: *I think he's wonderful, even if you don't.*

Charlie's father pretended to puff out his chest. "It was nothing, dear girl, nothing at all. A few minutes rest . . ." His eyes were on the burning house as sparks burst through the roof in a spectacular shower. "Will you look at that!" he said wonderingly. "Just look at that!"

"What were you doing in a closet, for pete's sake?" Charlie demanded. "Why'd you come out here in the first place?"

Rachel fingered the bow on the back of her sunbonnet. "I just wanted to talk to Katya," she said. "I wanted to tell her I was sorry she'd had such a terrible life. I thought I could make her understand that *her* contest was over a long time ago, and she ought to stop thinking about it. And I had plenty of time between the picture taking and the start of the parade . . ."

"That was dumb!" As happy as he was to have them both back, Charlie disliked his cousin at that moment. She really believed she could do anything, and she'd almost gotten his father and herself killed trying to prove it.

"Rachel wanted to put the poor old ghost to rest," John said tolerantly. "Or the poor young ghost. Whichever."

"I *know* it was dumb," Rachel retorted, "but it seemed like a good idea this morning. Anyway, Katya was waiting in the front hall when I went into the house. It was almost as if she was expecting me." Her eyes widened. "Do you think she *was* expecting me? Maybe that's why it seemed so logical to go to see her. Maybe she was willing me to come." She brushed the thought away. "Oh, it was awful! She grabbed me and pulled me up the stairs. She'd gotten younger again. She didn't look any older than I am now—but so strong! She dragged me into that room where we saw her dancing, and then into the closet. I tried to fight her off, but I just couldn't. She kept screaming that she was going to be the queen, and no one was going to stop her!"

"Even if it meant burning down the house with you in it," Charlie's father said. "Well, you did the right thing, kid. You made so much noise I didn't have to waste any time searching for you." He turned to Charlie. "I got the door open, and we took those back stairs in one—well, maybe two leaps. Didn't stop until we collapsed out there in the yard behind the house. Whoosh!" He lay back in the grass and stared up at the lead-colored sky. "Clouds look good to me," he said. "Everything looks good to me now. I never was so scared in my life."

"Katya rode on the queen's float in your place," Charlie told his cousin. "I saw her."

Rachel stared at him in amazement. "How could she do that?" she demanded. "Couldn't people see it wasn't me?"

"Not with a sunbonnet covering her face. I didn't know, myself, until I got up close to take a picture."

John sat up, clutching his bruised arm. He looked at this watch. "Listen, gang, we have to get back to the park. As I remember it, the parade stops at First and Clark for each band to do its stuff and show off a little. There'll be a reviewing stand set up, and the mayor will stop the action a few times to give awards to the best floats as they pass by. It's a slow business, but we're still going to have to hurry. There'll be a real commotion when the parade ends and people see they've been cheering the wrong queen." He clapped his hand to his forehead. "And the folks! Your grandmother's going to be waiting to see you, Rachel. What are we doing here when—"

Charlie grabbed his father's good arm. "Look!" he whispered hoarsely. "Over there—on the road!"

A slim figure in a brown gown and sunbonnet stood at the entrance to the clearing. Charlie heard Rachel's gasp and his father's exclamation. If he was dreaming, they were dreaming, too.

"She's back!" Rachel sounded as if she were going to scream. "Oh, Uncle John, what'll we do?"

"Sit still. Just sit still. It'll be all right."

Charlie wondered how his father could be so sure. They were looking at a ghost, an angry ghost who had tried to kill Rachel. Katya Torin had been insane for years. Her spirit might be capable of destroying them all.

The figure moved into the clearing, seeming to glide rather than walk. Charlie remembered that the ghost-girl had danced in the upstairs bedroom without leaving a mark on the dusty floor. There would be no footprints here, either, he thought, not even a bent grass blade.

Thunder rattled across the sky, nearer this time.

Rachel stirred as if she was getting ready to run. John put out a steadying hand.

"Wait," he whispered, "don't move."

The girl was close now. When she was a few feet away, she halted and faced the burning house. Then, very deliberately, she turned toward the watchers in the grass.

The face under the sunbonnet was young and quite beautiful. Charlie recognized the strong features, the olive skin, the curling dark hair. But the eyes had changed. When he'd seen Katya as an old lady, as a middle-aged woman, as a furious younger one, and as the queen looking down from her float, her eyes had been hard and glittering. Now they were serene.

"I rode in the parade," she said in a clear young voice. "Everybody cheered." She smiled contentedly before walking on toward the house.

"What's she going to do now?" Charlie didn't want to look, but he couldn't turn away. His father jumped up and then stopped as if he, too, were frozen by the girl's obvious intent. When she reached the porch, the heavy door burst open in fiery welcome, and Katya vanished inside.

There was nothing to say, nothing to do but leave. John helped Rachel to her feet. "Time to go, troops, " he said in a strained voice. "You okay, Rachel?"

Rachel nodded silently, her eyes wet with tears.

"Charlie?"

"I'm okay." He followed his father across the yard,

thinking of that slim, brown-clad figure walking into the fire.

As they climbed into the car, the rain began at last. Rachel leaned back and touched her sooty face. "I feel as if I've been to the moon and back," she murmured. "I feel unreal."

John backed the car and plunged into the lane without stopping for any last looks backward. "Gotta get our queen to her subjects," he said. "Gotta get Pike River's newest guitar player to the contest." He was trying to sound unconcerned, but his voice shook. His face was drawn under its layer of soot.

Charlie listened in disbelief. They'd just been through the strangest, most terrifying experience of their lives, and his father was already thinking about what was going to happen next. "You can't be in the contest," he said. "How can you play the guitar with a sore arm?"

John Hocking laughed. "Very tenderly," he retorted. "Don't be such a pessimist, Charlie. We've made it this far, and we'll manage what's ahead. One thing, though. I think we should agree to keep quiet about—about all this. What happened—it's over now. The ghost got what she wanted, and now she's gone and so is the house. I can't see any reason to get the town into an uproar when we can't prove a thing. Of course, if anybody else noticed it wasn't Rachel in the parade . . ." He frowned. "We'll see. I'd rather keep the whole business to ourselves. What do you say, Charlie?"

"Right," Charlie agreed. He wished his knees would stop shaking.

"Rachel?"

Rachel rammed the sunbonnet on her head and peered out at them. "Right," she said. "But I really do feel weird."

EPILOGUE

Charlie wanted to walk. He promised his family he'd meet them at the softball diamond at nine to see the fireworks, and then he took off into the dark, enjoying deep breaths of rain-washed air.

It had been a pretty good day, considering the way it had begun. Rachel had stepped with typical Rachel determination into her role as Sunbonnet Queen. After a fast stop at home to clean up—Rachel showered, John washed at the kitchen sink, and Charlie brushed spot remover on the white collar and cuffs of the queen's costume—they'd arrived at the park just as Grandma Lou was bustling around the log-cabin float. She'd apparently been asking people if they'd seen her granddaughter, and she was starting to panic. Rachel had climbed quickly to the cabin door and posed there, so Grandma could see how the queen had looked during the parade. Her smile was forced, her expression glazed, but she waved at the people milling around the float and even blew a kiss. Charlie marveled. When they'd reached the park, Rachel had told him she felt as if she were going to throw up.

From twelve until two Charlie had helped Grandma and Grandpa at the hotdog stand. That had been fun, but as soon as the crowd began to thin out, he had slipped away to look for his father. It had seemed important to know where everyone was.

He found his father, pale but cheerful, watching Rachel award balloons to the winners of the three-legged race. John admitted his shoulder was too sore to play his guitar in the contest, but he'd volunteered to act as master of ceremonies and be one of the judges. Charlie walked with him to the bandstand.

As he sat in the audience and listened to his father's patter, Charlie felt as if he were discovering something important. The only reason his father had believed the truth about Katya Torin—*the only reason he'd been there in time to save Rachel's life*—was because he was a special kind of person. Childlike. Trusting. Ready to believe the unbelievable. Another grown-up—even Grandpa Will—would have doubted, wanted proof, until it was too late.

"Hey there, kid. Mind some company?"

Charlie came back to the present with a start. His father was ambling toward him, whistling "Dinah" as he cut across the grass. He'd bought a new straw hat from a peddler to replace the one he'd lost in the fire, and he looked as jaunty as ever.

"Kind of nice, walking in the dark," he commented as he fell in step next to Charlie. "You know, when I was a kid growing up in this town, I thought it was the dullest place in the world. Now I'm glad to be back. On a night like this anything seems possible."

Charlie sighed. All afternoon he'd felt his dream of life in California slipping away. Thoughts of Jake Fisher's swimming class had flickered through his mind. He imagined himself playing a trumpet, or a trombone, and marching with the Pike River Middle School band. He had even wondered what it would be like to go cross-country skiing with his father during a long Wisconsin winter.

On a night like this anything seems possible.

There was a sharp *crack,* and a shower of silver and red burst across the sky.

"Hey, how about that!" John exclaimed. "A whole fleet of unidentified flying objects!"

"It's just the fireworks starting," Charlie said automatically. Then he decided he liked his father's idea better.

ABOUT THE AUTHOR

BETTY REN WRIGHT's short stories have appeared in *Redbook, Ladies' Home Journal, Young Miss,* and many other magazines. Her book *The Dollhouse Murders* was a 1983 Edgar Award nominee in the best juvenile category, and winner of the Texas Bluebonnet Award. *Christina's Ghost* also won the Texas Bluebonnet Award. Her other books include *A Ghost in the Window, The Summer of Mrs. MacGregor, Ghosts Beneath Our Feet, The Secret Window,* and *Getting Rid of Marjorie* (all Apple Paperbacks).

An enthusiastic angler, grandmother, and cat and dog owner, Ms. Wright lives in Kenosha, Wisconsin, with her husband, a painter.